A Week in the Future

Catherine Helen Spence

Serialised in *The Centennial Magazine: An Australian Monthly*
December 1888-July 1889

CHAPTER I

Introductory

I have often observed that unmarried people, old maids and old bachelors, take a keener interest in old family history, and in the ramifications of the successive generations from the most remote ancestors they can claim, than those who form the actual links in the chain of descent, and leave children behind them to carry on the chronicle. Having lived all my life with a mother who nearly attained the age of a century, and having a strong interest in things past as well as in things present, I have been steeped in memories of old times. I know how middle-class intelligent people lived and worked, dressed and dined, worshipped God and amused themselves, what they read for pleasure and for profit, not only so far as her own recollections could carry the dear old lady, but two generations farther back. In her youth she had lived much with an intelligent grandmother, who could recollect the rebellion of 1745, and the battle of Prestonpans, and had been of mature years during the American War of Independence.

My own mother's youth had been the period of the gigantic struggle of Great Britain, sometimes single-handed, against the power of the first Napoleon. The older lady had said to her then youthful descendant that no one could expect to see as much as she had seen in her life, which extended from 1734 to 1817, and included the American War, the French Revolution, and the application of machinery to so many of the arts. The grandchild, born at the beginning of 1791, had seen five French Revolutions, and the map of Europe strangely altered; triumphs of art and science, countless in number; steam, gas, electricity, the railway system; mechanical inventions which had revolutionized industry; and the rise of mighty colonies to compensate for the loss of the United States. In the growth of one great colony she had taken a deep personal interest, for she had watched it from the day of very small things in 1839. As we sat and talked together, we would wonder what there could be for me to see that would be equal to what had unfolded before her eyes. Was there to be federation or disintegration? Was the homogeneous yet heterogeneous British Empire to be firmly welded together, or were the component parts to be allowed peacefully to separate and form new states? Was the *régime* of unrestricted competition and free trade and individualism to be kept up, or were these to be exchanged for protection and collectivism? What was to be the outcome of the Irish Question, of German Socialism, of Russian Nihilism? Was Britain to remain mistress of India, and to keep that dependency? Was she to annex all territory which might be supposed to preserve her open route towards it? What struggle was there to be in central Asia between Britain and Russia? What power was likely to demolish the terrible armed peace of Europe? Such questions as these occupied my own mind primarily--my mother had taken the keenest interest in them all, but latterly she cared less for the questions of the day, and as her health gradually declined, she went further and further back till she seemed to live more in the first ten years of the century than in the more recent past.

When, after a long, wearing, and painful illness, I closed my mother's eyes--my companionship and occupation both gone at once--I had to consider how I was to take up my life again. I was poorer after her death, because her annuity, which must have made the insurance company the losers, died with her, and I was left with that sort of provision which the world considers quite sufficient for an elderly single woman.

My brother Robert came the day after the funeral to talk matters over with me. "You have had a shock, Emily," he said, "You would not save yourself any way;--now, you must try to take life easier. What do you yourself think of doing?"

"I mean to stay on here if I can manage it," I said.

"Don't attempt to keep house by yourself, it is too expensive, and too much of a tie. Of course, so long as our mother lived, you had to keep a home for her, and to stay in it, but now, if you will not come and live with us, you had better go and board somewhere, or furnish a set of apartments, and that would leave you at liberty. You have not work now for two servants; if you have only one you cannot leave her by herself in the house. Belle says she supposes I cannot persuade you to take up your abode with us."

CHAPTER I

My sister-in-law, though in her way an excellent woman, was one of the most abject slaves of Mrs. Grundy, and her ways were not my ways. Their house seemed as full as it could rightly be with their own large family, and I could not in conscience think to occupy their only decent spare room, at present tenanted by the married daughter and her first baby. I was not disposed to go to a little den which did duty for a stray bachelor guest. I clung to a home of my own.

"I dislike boarding-houses and furnished apartments," I said. "After being virtually the head of a house so long, I do not care to be a mere pecuniary convenience to any one. I want a home to which I can invite my friends, where I can have company or quiet as I please."

"My dear Emily," said Robert, "A single woman in your circumstances should be quite satisfied if she has two or three comfortably furnished apartments, and can invite a few friends to tea occasionally."

"That means that I am to be shut out henceforward from the company of men, for the tea guests are always women."

"Of course, gentlemen all dine late, and do not appreciate even afternoon tea much; but the social evenings of our youth are no more. You recollect Emily? 'Come to tea and spend the evening.' Ah! those were pleasant times. A little music and singing, a carpet dance, round games, and flirtation. But you are past the age for that sort of thing. I did not think you would care now for the disturbing male element in society."

"I want to mix with people who are in the world, and engaged in its business. I have for years devoted myself to my mother, now I should like to live my own natural life for a few years."

"You will get far more real information as to how the world goes on from books than from any male guests you can induce to visit you at no end of expense. I am sure the dinner guests whom we entertain, and whom Belle and I meet elsewhere, do not give us any new ideas or much refreshment. If I were you I should be glad of the peaceful life before you, after all you have gone through lately; with books and needlework, and your piano, and a little committee work such as your soul loveth, in conjunction with a number of bright practical women. Or suppose you get one of your friends to join you in housekeeping. That would be pleasant, and make things easier for you. There's Mary Bell, I dare say she would be glad to do it."

"I like Mary Bell very well, but I do not like her people, who would of course be constantly coming and going."

"Everywhere there is a lion in the path--I repeat it, Emily, I would gladly change with you. What between the mill of business, which is grinding exceedingly small in these days in the way of profit--protection and the working man have it all their own way now--and the mill of social requirements, and the mill of family anxieties, life is hardly worth living. As for the young people, after we have got them brought up and educated our troubles seem only to begin. There is Frank spending all his salary, and all I allow him besides, and always in debt, because he will bet on races and play for high stakes with insufficient skill; and Gerald, dangling after a girl in a restaurant who I fear will hook him,--the two boys are not much comfort; and Florrie, who is more than half afraid to go back to the station, and I'm sure Belle will have a sore heart to part from her. Who would think that Alf. Henderson was a secret drunkard, and that the delicate health that won Florrie's compassion was the consequence of his own bad habits. And Jeannie has set her heart on a man who has no merit whatever but that of being a good tennis player and having a fine voice. There is no rise in him. The four younger ones may do better, but you never can tell. I often feel as if a large family was a mistake--at any rate now-a-days, when so much is expected from parents."

I was very sorry for my brother's family troubles, but I felt as if he and his wife had lived too much for society and position, and had not taken the intelligent interest in their children, in studying their tastes and guarding against their weaknesses, which might have saved some disappointments. Belle, I knew, had been carried away by Mr. Henderson's large possessions, and had disregarded some ominous signs in her future son-in-law.

I thought Robert rather cold-blooded in his advice that I should wrench myself from the old home where I had taken root, but the more I thought over ways and means, I became the more afraid that he had sound reason on his side. I, however, delayed advertising my house. I put off the evil day till I could accustom my mind to the change.

A singular feeling of malaise oppressed me, I missed the engrossing occupation of the last two years, and I did not recover the spring and elasticity of body and mind which I had expected. It was on one of those suddenly hot days which we have in an Australian August that I had walked rather far and rather fast, and when I got home, tired and breathless, I found Florrie Henderson come to say good-bye before she went with her little baby boy, Hugh, to the station. Florrie threw herself into my arms in an hysterical passion of tears, and I, instead of being able to comfort her or steady her nerves, fainted away for the first time in my life. Florrie's alarm about me made her throw off for the time her own trouble; she sent for Dr. Brown, and meantime used all the simple and ordinary remedies for restoration; but I had scarcely recovered full possession of my faculties when he arrived. Dr. Brown had been the wise and kind adviser of my mother, and he had often suggested that my devotion to her should be less absorbing, and predicted that I should suffer from the strain. He had even practised some auscultation from time to time, which he now proceeded to repeat more minutely, and he questioned me closely on my sensations and symptoms. I could read his countenance like a book, and could understand his little impatient gestures and half-uttered words. I felt that there was something seriously wrong.

"Tell me the truth," I said. "It is the heart?"

"Yes, just the weak part of you, which I have been anxious about all through this long nursing of Mrs. Bethel."

"And it is serious?"

"Serious? Why, that is according how you take it?"

"I take it literally. It is organic?"

"Yes, organic--but you know with ease and a quiet life, such as you may lead now, there is no immediate danger."

CHAPTER I

"I may live--how long? Don't be afraid to tell me the truth."

"You will live a year, perhaps two, with great care. You will need to be very careful."

"I know what that means," said I, bitterly. "I must give up all the things that make life worth living, all the outside interests that are the very bread of life to a solitary spinster, all the larger objects which the best and noblest of my brothers and sisters are striving to accomplish and absorb myself in the one idea of self-preservation."

"Oh, Auntie," said Florrie, who with wet eyes and choking sobs had listened to the death-warrant pronounced by our old, experienced, and kindly family physician. "You must take care for all our sakes. Think how valuable even two years of your life is to many who love and honor you."

"Yes, valuable so long as it is life," I said, "but of no value whatever if I shut myself up in my shell, and merely absorb nutriment and warmth, and exclude all disturbing influences--the wind of heaven and the cares and labors of earth."

"I did not pass so sweeping a sentence, Miss Bethel," said Dr. Brown. "You are only to avoid all over fatigue, all excitement, and especially all worry."

"What is life without these things?" I asked vehemently.

"It is what all old people have to do," said Dr. Brown kindly.

"And was it not this that my poor mother felt so hard? Half her misery was occasioned by ennui. The regret that she could do nothing for herself or for anyone else embittered the last two years of her life. And if even she, at the age of ninety-seven, chafed at the life of inaction and helplessness, what must I do? I am not old; I have not been severed from life and all its interests gradually by the chilling of my sensations and the weakening of my faculties. I can see, hear, speak, learn, observe, reflect, aspire, as well as I ever could do in my life, and to have to die before I have seen the problems which have puzzled me

CHAPTER I 8

all my life solved, or nearly solved, is to me very hard."

"Dear Auntie," said Florrie with a broken, tremulous voice, yet musical, as her voice always was when she quoted from her beloved Tennyson:--

"To thee, dear, doubtless will be given A life that bears immortal fruit, In such high offices as suit The full-grown energies of Heaven."

"Doubtless--is it doubtless? And even if these high offices were indeed assured to me, it is here on earth that I am passionately interested. How foreign to me with my present nature are the cares and employments of a disembodied spirit, moving about among other equally unsubstantial spirits, or at best reclothed in some strange new personality. It is this world that I have loved and will continue to love," I said passionately, to the surprise of my two listeners.

"I should have thought that you of all women sat loose to the world," said Dr. Brown. "And so should I," said my niece, "Mother always says Aunt Emily is the most unworldly person she ever knew, though not in the least sanctimonious either."

"In a certain sense I do sit loose to the world, but I know and feel convinced by many signs that we are on the eve of a great social and industrial revolution. I had hoped to have seen some outcome from the groaning and travailing of all creation, and from the efforts of so many earnest and devoted men and women for the amelioration of the conditions under which the toiling masses live and labor. What will come out of Irish Agitation, German Socialism, Russian Nihilism? Will India be prepared for self-government? Is the mighty Chinese Empire really awaking? When and how is the barbarous practice of war to be abolished? Is the scarcely less deadly war between labor and capital to end peacefully, or is the cut-throat competition for cheapness all over the world to be ended by a terrible and destructive catastrophe? Is religion to become more Catholic or more sectarian? What is a year or a problematical two years of life, wrapped up in cotton wadding, to my eager questioning soul? I would give the year or two of life you promise me for ONE WEEK IN THE FUTURE. A solid week I mean. Not a glance like a momentary vision, but one week--seven days and nights to live with the generations who are to come, to see all their doings, and to breathe in their atmosphere, so as to imbibe their real spirit."

"How far in the future should you like to spend your solid week--twenty years, fifty years, a hundred years hence?" said Dr. Brown, with a curious expression on his intelligent countenance.

"You know, Florrie, I have often said to you and to other people that I would give anything to see the world fifty years after I left it, but as I am not to live such a long life as my mother's by thirty-five years, and not even the Psalmist's measure of three score and ten, and as the changes that have to be wrought may take a long time, I think I should prefer a hundred years to elapse before I see my WEEK IN THE FUTURE!"

"But everybody whom you knew and cared about would be dead," said Florrie. "I should not feel the least interest in the world after a century. A hundred years--it is like an eternity."

"Like an eternity to twenty-six, but it is only three years longer than your grandmother's single life."

"That saw great changes certainly," said Dr. Brown, "and the progress of events, as you must have observed, becomes more rapid with each decade; I should myself hesitate between fifty years and a hundred--fifty has the advantage which Mrs. Henderson feels so strongly of greater familiarity and possible personal survivals, but a hundred years must work radical changes, more startling, and possibly--I only say possibly--more interesting."

More interesting to me, I feel sure. And Florrie, my affections strike back to remote ancestors and would strike onward to remote collateral descendants, which are all that an old maid can have. Why, Florrie, I might see little Hugh's children and grand-children in the flesh."

"Then," said Dr. Brown, "you elect to overleap a complete century. And how would you like to see the world of the latter end of the twentieth century. Like Asmodeus, by unroofing the houses and spying on the doings and misdoings of the *post nati*, or like a beneficent spirit, hovering over the cities and fields, watching the human ants in the nest, or the bees in the hive, or the butterflies among the flowers, and listening to the words you hear them speak, yourself invisible and unheard."

"No, not like a spirit at all, but just in this habit as I am, like a middle-aged or rather an elderly single woman, who surely can never be altogether out of date in any century"

"And *where* would you prefer to have your peep? In Melbourne, in London, in your Scotch ancestral home, in New York, or in Pekin?"

"Every place has its charms, but as the older countries are those where the greater need of change exists, let me be located in or close to London."

"Pekin represents an older civilization," argued Dr. Brown.

"But too unfamiliar to be as interesting as the British metropolis. I need all my past knowledge to throw light on the new revelations. The language, the literature, the history, and the traditions of England are among my most cherished possessions. A week of London for me."

"And who will give you to drink of mandragora that you may sleep away that gap of time, and traverse, not spiritually, but in the flesh, so many thousand miles of land and ocean?" asked Dr. Brown.

"Who but you, with your strong leaning towards the occult and the transcendental which are the favorite study of your leisure hours?"

"Are you really serious?" said Dr. Brown more gravely

"Perfectly serious."

"It is because you believe it to be impossible that you would barter a year, or it may be two, dating from August, 1888 for a single week in 1988. It would really be like all the bargains recorded by tradition or supersitition between man and the arch enemy of souls, always greatly the worse for the human party to the transaction. Why, at best, it would be fifty-two to one."

"Not so," said I, "for I should barter a year or two of failing health and disappointed hopes for a week of full life and intellectual satisfaction. I should save my friends from all trouble and anxiety on my behalf. I should at the same time save myself from the temptation to peevish repining and exacting selfishness. I have not received your death-warrant with the meekness and resignation which I know you expected from me. I do not feel as if I could bear to watch the slow closing in of life for myself, just after I have watched it for the being dearest to me in the world, especially with the strong hold on life I have within me at present. It puts me in mind of the terrible story I read when I was a girl, in a *Blackwood's Magazine*, of a political offender who was seized by the relentless arm of despotic power, and shut up in a strong prison with thirteen windows. During the first night, by some devilish machinery, one window was closed, and next day there was but twelve, the next day eleven, and so on till at last the *coup de grâce* was given, and life was crushed out of him simultaneously with the closing of the last window."

"But Auntie," said Florrie, softly, "you have always said life was good. Father calls you an optimist. Mother says you always see the best side of things and of people."

"Yes, life has been good--very good. Like Harriett (sic) Martineau, I feel I have had a good share of life hitherto, but that has been because I have taken an active part in it, and it has been and continues to be so exceedingly interesting, but I should not like to linger on the scene when I can be no longer serviceable."

"It shows how differently life is held by different people. If I had to deal with your mother, Florrie, she would think a year or two with her husband and children a vast deal better than a week, better than ten years elsewhere," said Dr. Brown.

"Belle knows they would be all only too happy to have the privilege of nursing her, and that they would do anything to prolong her valuable life," said I.

CHAPTER I

"Oh Auntie, how glad I should be to take you with me to the station. It is said to be so healthy, and is not exciting, and I'd be so glad of your society, for mother won't let Jeannie go, but--," and Florrie sighed; she had to reckon up a master of the house who was not reasonable, and was not well disposed to his wife's family. "But anyhow you must not stay here alone, you must go to live with your own near and dear relatives. Do not speak as if you had nobody to whom your life is precious."

"I do not say that, Florrie, my dear, but though I have kind relatives and dear friends, there is now no one to whom I am indispensable. Indeed, I am doubtful if any of us is so indispensable as he or she fancies to any one, but I always prayed that I might live while my mother needed me, and that at least has been given."

"I fear I should have to live longer than Dr. Brown's utmost limit of two years to see that consummation. Your parents' consent must first be given," said I.

"I think they are a little moved now they see money is not everything."

"But Claude has to make his way, and it will take a long while before he can earn an income sufficient for an extravagant girl like Jeannie and the lot of you. Perhaps my death might help Jeannie better than my life."

"Don't say so, Auntie, and please don't call us extravagant. Father says we are, but it isn't really true."

"I don't know what you call extravagant, but you girls each spend as much on your dress and personal expenses as my father gave to his three girls, and he was called liberal. It is a pity, however, that the requirements of modern society make marriage, instead of the hand-in-hand travel up the hill which it ought to be, a goal to be attained when the hill is climbed, unless a young man inherits unearned money."

"And then it often is a curse," said Florrie bitterly.

"In most cases it is the culmination of a young man's ambition to be able to afford to marry a young woman of education and refined tastes. How much better for happiness and morality if it were to be the natural first step in the life of an industrious, steady young man," I said.

"That opens out large questions, Miss Bethel," said Dr. Brown. "Will people see things differently a hundred years hence?"

"Anyhow, Florrie, I cannot live to see Jeannie married, but she has my best wishes. I like Claude Moore, and believe he has far more grit in him than your father or mother can see just now. And Claude and Jeannie love each other, which is the main point. He must work hard, and she must reduce her ideas of an establishment to what is obtainable on moderate means. But now, Florrie, I must really send you home. You must leave Dr. Brown to prescribe something, for though I am set down as incurable, of course it would be unprofessional not to give the chemist a turn, though I dare say I would do as well with wholesome neglect and the expectancy treatment. Come, dear, it must be good-bye."

Her hot tears fell on my cheek as she kissed me. As she went out at the door she met the postman, who brought no letters for me, but one of those tradesmen's circulars which are the daily annoyance of modern life, and a book sent from England by my dear old friend Mrs. Durant. Florrie came back with the packet in her hand which she proceeded to untie.

"I hope it is a good new novel to cheer you up. By the by, thanks for the *Children of Gibeon* for my birthday, Auntie. This is not a novel, however, but a book on Scientific Meliorism and the Evolution of Happiness, by Jane Hume Clapperton. Let me have it when you have done with it. The subject is one after your own heart. I must say good-bye really now. However, you really look better than you did."

Dr. Brown had taken the book out of my niece's hand, and glanced rapidly at the running titles on the top of the pages. "I think this will give you some speculative ideas about your week in the future. I shall prescribe, along with a necessary sedative, the careful reading of this book."

CHAPTER I

I was indeed deeply interested in the book, I half forgot my own impending fate as I saw what this hopeful writer had gathered from other authors and other observers, and had worked out for herself from the signs of the times into a foreshadowing of the society of the future. Dr. Brown gave me two days to read the book and then called to see how I was.

"You are better, decidedly better;' he said.

"Not organically better, however?"

"No I cannot say that, but you have been agreeably interested and diverted from the shock of two days ago."

"It is because I have been living so much in the future."

"Still harping on the future," said the doctor. "Are you still serious about your solid week."

"Quite so, still more eager than ever since I have read this book."

"Then will you put yourself in my hands, and I shall try what I can do to further your wishes."

"I am all obedience and submission," I said.

"Give your maid a week's holiday, and tell her you are going for a little change of air and scene. Pack up a few necessaries in a hand-bag. I can wait for you, you are no dawdler."

I said what was needed to Janet, who was overjoyed at a week's holiday, and promised to take the key of the house with a message to my brother. I could not have written a note to save my life. I changed my dress, and packed my Gladstone bag with more rapidity than was quite prudent, considering the state of my heart, and I stepped into the doctor's brougham with a curious feeling of expectancy. I was taken last in his rounds that day, and driven not to his own home, but to a private hospital for patients from the country in which he had a large interest, and introduced to a quiet room at the back.

"Now," said he, "the main thing is strength of volition on your own part, aided by all the power of will I can lend you. This *Week in the Future* is what you long for more than all things--all other objects are excluded by this over-mastering desire. Lie down on this couch with your bag in your hands. Your appearance, if we succeed in our great experiment, will be that of trance or suspended animation, and that is what I shall call it to the nurse in attendance."

I obeyed Dr. Brown's instructions. I did not know what to expect, but I knew what I wished.

"Are you ready for your wonderful journey?" said he, making passes over me. I could just see him in the midst of this performance take out of his waistcoat pocket a small phial containing a colorless liquid.

"Ready?"

"Quite ready," I whispered. I had not power to speak above my breath.

He poured out the contents into a wine glass, diluted them with a little water, and held the potion to my lips, supporting my head on his left hand.

"Drink and wish."

I drank, and felt a singular calm come over me for a space, it might have been a few moments, it might have been a whole minute, but it was ineffably sweet, all the malaise, and restlessness had gone--I was at peace. Then came a mighty spasm like what I could conceive death to be. This life was closed to me. I was no longer on the little couch in the private hospital with Dr. Brown bending over me, but standing on my feet with my hand-bag on my arm. I was not in Adelaide or Australia, but as I had wished to be in the old country, in that England I had loved so well, which I had left, indeed, at the age of thirteen, but which I had revisited twenty-five years after in the full maturity of my powers of observation and in the full glow of my womanly sympathies. This was a suburb of London, a north-west suburb so far as I could guess. If so removed as to place, was there not a chance that the still greater removal as to time was also granted me?

CHAPTER II

MONDAY

Associated Homes

It was Friday afternoon when I took leave of life in Adelaide, South Australia. It was on a Monday morning that I woke, and began the strange experience of a *Week in the Future*. The first thing I was fully conscious of was that I had completely thrown off all the uncomfortable sensations as well as the apprehensions of the last two days. I was not indeed young, but I was well and strong, and full of life, energy, and hope. I stood--as I said before--in the open air. I felt the soft moist climate of the father-land caressing me; the sun shone, not with the summer blaze of our Australian skies, but as if through a tender haze. Yes! this was London that lay vast, but strangely changed before me. Where was the smoke? Was smoke one of the exploded nuisances of the past? The gas lamps familiar to me were replaced by something new--probably some modification of the electric light, for I could not conceive of anything better being invented even in a hundred years, and I hoped and almost felt that I had bridged over that length of time. And now I seemed to see difficulties in my way. How could I, a stranger from another hemisphere and from another century, ask for information, and learn what I longed so much to know without subjecting myself to suspicions of lying and imposture? How hard it would be to keep silent, and simply watch for the changes which must have taken place in the way of living and thinking since men lived and thought a hundred years before. I did not like to stand like a fool or an idler, and I began to walk briskly along a suburban street which I seemed to know, but it had no longer rows of houses placed closely together, but large buildings, each standing in extensive grounds. Passers-by looked well-to-do; their clothes varied a good deal in fashion more than material. A workman--erect, strong, and cheery, with a bag of tools on his shoulder, whistling sweetly a tune quite unknown to me--was moving towards a large building, which lay on the east side of the street. It was like a palace for size, but not palatial in its style of architecture, which was plain and simple. Garden plots lay in front of it, and a beautiful lawn, while I could see that there were many acres of cultivated ground at the back.

CHAPTER II

"Good morning, Sir," I said to the workman. "Good morning, madam," he replied. "It is a very fine morning;' I ventured to say. Surely the weather could not be quite a worn out topic of conversation in the variable climate of England--even after the lapse of a hundred years.

"Yes, it is fine after yesterday's rain. It came on handsomely and no mistake. Bad for the harvest!"

"Are you going to work here?" said I.

"Yes, we have the contract for repairs at the Owen Home here; the rain got in at the north wing; the first leak there for ten years, I hear; but it is a rare strong old building."

I saw inscribed over the gateway in deep cut stone letters "Owen Associated Home, 1900". Yes, I might have lived to have heard of the new departure, if I had not seen it in the colonies, if I had lived twelve years longer.

I walked with the workman to the door, which stood open and showed a handsome entrance hall enclosed. We both touched the knob of a bell I supposed to be electric. A young woman came to our summons, and directed, in the first place, the workman to his job, and then asked me whom I wished to see.

"Does Mrs. Carmichael live here?" I said, as if by inspiration.

"Yes, madam; No. 7," was the reply. "I think she is in her own room. I shall ascertain if she objects to be disturbed."

"If not, give her my card, and say 'Miss Emily Bethel would be happy to see her.'"

A question, telephonic, answered at once, let me know that Mrs. Carmichael would be equally happy to see me. The attendant motioned me to a lift, and stepped in after me, and in a few seconds we were on the second floor, and walked along a corridor till we reached No. 7, when she took my card

CHAPTER II

MISS BETHEL ADELAIDE, S.A.

to the occupant of the room. A pleasant voice said "Come in," and the young woman left me to pursue her own avocation. I entered a large, light, airy, comfortable apartment, one half of which was furnished as a bedroom, and the other half as a sitting-room. The weather was a little chill outside after the rain, though the month was August, but there was no fireplace visible, though the room was pleasantly warm. A pleasant-faced lady of apparently my own age, though I afterwards discovered that she was considerably older, was sitting in an easy chair by a table, with her work and work-basket--quite like the old lady of our own day.

"Sit down, pray," and she placed me on a sofa, close to her chair. "I am indeed very glad to welcome a cousin from over the sea. We do not see so much of our far-away kinsfolk as we should like. I have of course the newspapers and books, but I have long wanted to hear by word of mouth what these great southern lands which our forefathers planted have attained to."

"And, alas, I cannot tell you," said I, plunging at once, *in medias res*, "my knowledge of Australia is, unfortunately, of old date."

"I am at a loss to reconcile this with your card, which puts down Adelaide as your present residence."

"We are now, I presume," I said making another desperate stroke, "in the month of August, 1988."

"Just so," said Mrs. Carmichael, with a surprised look at the assertion.

"My last knowledge of Melbourne, and indeed of the world, ended in August, 1888."

The lady looked at me as if questioning my sanity, but I stood her gaze steadily. "I have exchanged a year of life for a Week in the Future, and I chose to have my week a century ahead of the date of the bargain. I have been permitted to make the exchange, and now with your good help I want to make the most and the best of my short span of existence."

"We are very sceptical of the supernatural now-a-days," said Mrs. Carmichael.

"Not more so than I have been," said I, earnestly. "I cannot account for the extraordinary position in which I find myself, which is indeed staggering to my own powers of belief, and must be tenfold more so to a stranger, though you appear to be a remote kinsman, and might be disposed to believe what is so marvellous. It may be that the intense longing I had to know what was in the womb of time and ready to be delivered, has projected me over nearly half the globe, and the lapse of a complete century--more than three average generations. I may be now in a mere trance or vision. This room, this Owen Home may be a mere phantasm or mirage, and you a mere eidolon--an appearance--a shadow thrown out by my own inner consciousness, or like a dream, which evades you when you try to grasp it."

"Nothing so unsubstantial," said Mrs. Carmichael, "if there is anything unreal or shadowy in presence it is yourself. You will find all things altogether solid and coherent with us twentieth century people. If it is indeed as you say, and you have no knowledge of recent matters, I think it is likely that your week will be as satisfactory to yourself as it will be most interesting to me. Be my guest for this week, at least as far as it will serve your purpose and satisfy your desire to know all that can be known about our life in the short space at your command."

I accepted this kind offer with gratitude, though I was not at all sure that Mrs. Carmichael believed the strange story I told.

"I feel as anxious to know about the life in the past as you can possibly be to learn about our present time."

"That is impossible," said I. "Books can tell you all about us and our doings, while to all of us in all generations the future is a blank."

"Perhaps we are too much engaged with the works of our own day to give sufficient attention to the records of the past, at least I notice this is the case with the young people. And things are so much changed from the days of ferment and unrest which you speak of, that it is difficult for them to understand the language and the temper of the times. It needs to be, as it were, translated to them, for they carry their pre-conceived impressions into the books of old times. At least that is what my son-in-law--who is a literary man and somewhat of an antiquarian--says. For myself, I lived much with my grandmother, and she used to tell me of the old days, and, old-lady-like, occasionally regretted them; though, on the whole, she thought things much more equitably managed under the new *régime*.

"Who then was your grandmother?" I asked eagerly.

"She was from Adelaide in Australia, and that is why my heart warmed to your name and address when I saw it on your card. Her name was Florence Bethel before her marriage. My father was the eldest and only surviving child of her unhappy first marriage."

"Then your father was the little baby Hugh I knew as a baby."

"His name was Hugh. He was a very good son to my grandmother."

"And had poor Florrie--it seems disrespectful to speak thus of your venerable grandmother," I said, laughing, "but I parted from Florrie in the bloom of her youth a few days ago, and she will always be Florrie to me--had she a happier fate in her second marriage after that wretched creature (I must call your grandfather names, too) had departed this life?"

"He did not die. They lived separated for many years, and at last she got a divorce. Now-a-days it would have been much more promptly granted. She married again, happily, so far as I knew, but had no children. I recollect grandfather (as I called him) very well. He was very much attached to his step-son."

"Then you are really my dear Florrie's grand-daughter in the flesh. Did she ever speak of me, and of her grandmother who lived to be nearly a hundred."

CHAPTER II

"I have often heard her speak of the old lady, a very storehouse of memories."

"But not of me," said I, with considerable feeling. I think, seeing that my *amour propre* was touched, convinced Mrs. Carmichael of my identity, and of the truth of my story more than anything else. "Oh, yes! certainly, of you who showed so much sympathy with her troubles--the dear Aunt Emily who died within a fortnight of the grandmother. Oh! that was another link of association with your card!"

"It is a curious relationship," said I.

"We are sisters, rather than anything else more distant," said Mrs. Carmichael.

This was better than looking on my senior as my great grand niece. I felt strangely drawn to the kindly old lady, and more hopeful of getting the information I wanted from her than from others who knew less and cared less about the past. Nevertheless, even with her, there were difficulties. I scarcely knew where to begin, and said so.

"You must ask questions for yourself, as well as take note with your eyes, and pick up information casually. Things as they are, are so familiar to us that we scarcely know what is new and what is old, but my son-in-law could help you a good deal."

"I see a great change in the establishment of Associated Homes, for, I suppose, this is only one amongst many."

"They are all but universal now-a-days. This, however, was one of the oldest in the country, and our founders gave to it the name of the pioneer in the movement."

"The experiments of Robert Owen and of Fourier, and others, were only partially successful, but, considering the materials they had to build with, it was wonderful how much they effected, and they led the way to something better, I suppose?"

CHAPTER II

"Yes! We all acknowledge a deep debt of gratitude to these devoted men. The general breaking up of the old isolated homes, and the formation of the Associated or Unitary Homes, was due in the first place to the domestic servant difficulty. It was the middle classes who made the first start. The rich could always command sufficient domestic service by the high wages, by the luxurious living, and many privileges they could give. The working people who needed it even more did not understand the economy and the benefits of combination, till they were shown the example by the class above them, who had more education, and manners and tempers more under control. Now, of course, all the community are educated up to this standard, and all derive the full benefit of 'Associated Homes?

"How many families live in this house?" I asked.

"Twenty is our number."

"And I suppose they are of the professional and mercantile classes; not the working classes."

"We scarcely speak of the working classes now-a-days, for all of us work. Still I understand what you mean. Here live twenty families, descended from many generations of educated people--many of these still cherishing relics of past days, as you see in this apartment of mine."

"And these twenty families," said I, "would in old times have each inhabited a home--which they accounted their castle. Each with at least two sitting-rooms, several bedrooms, including one spare room for guests, and must have kept from one to three servants, according to their means and the number and ages of the family--an average of two servants in England, if not in Australia. Whereas you"--

"Well, when twenty families combine, the forty or fifty small sitting-rooms are exchanged,--the twenty dining-rooms for two large well-heated but uncarpeted eating-rooms or refectories; the twenty drawing-rooms, kept mostly for show, are represented by a large music room, an art room, a whist and chess room, a smoking room, a dancing room, a large library, a mechanics' room, and a ladies' work

CHAPTER II

room. Twenty families would have at least ten nurseries--we manage with two, and class rooms for the earlier education of children before they go to the public schools."

"And as for sleeping accommodation?" I asked.

"We have sleeping rooms to accommodate the twenty families comfortably, arranged in suites--with some few rooms for guests. Casual hospitality is frequent and inexpensive. There is a *pro rata* charge for each guest, and the table is always abundant, and the company pleasant, and some congenial amusement open to people of ordinary tastes. My grandmother used to tell me that one of the trials of life was the arrival of a guest to a shabby dinner."

"There was not much chance of that at her father's house. Belle was a most liberal housekeeper."

"Things went badly with them afterwards, I think; she also told me of the dinner-parties and the evening-parties which cost so much, both in money and trouble, and I did not think that they gave pleasure in proportion."

"Then how do you manage about servants?" I asked.

"The service in this as in similar homes is done by contract. The men and women who provide for the daily comfort of our lives are as independent and as much respected as those they wait upon. I think all our attendants here are members of Associated Homes of their own, except two who are engaged to sleep on the premises."

"And how many do you keep?"

"Mr. Oliphant (my son-in-law) who is one of the home committee, could give you more exact information. I think there are sixteen in all, and the washing is done in the home. We have every sort of labor-saving machinery that ingenuity can devise, or money can pay for, because the human instrument is far more costly than it ever was."

"Then, perhaps, your servants are as rich as you are yourselves?"

CHAPTER II

"I do not know, probably they are; but yet the service does not cost each family nearly as much as it did in the old times, there are fewer of them to keep, and there is no waste."

"The item of washing, thrown in, must make a difference to a London household certainly. But what do you ladies do with no housekeeping to attend to?"

"We are relieved from these cares, at least such of us are not on the house committee of three, elected yearly, who give a general supervision, and so we are set free to pursue the breadwinning avocation which all men and women must betake themselves."

"And how does the Associated Home answer for domestic comfort?" I asked. "The average Englishman as I knew him would rather be dull and cramped in a home where he was entirely master, than better lodged and served where he must give way on all sides to other people. The average Englishwoman fancied her mission was to practice housekeeping, and rule over her establishment of children and servants. Is not this combined home of yours too like the hotel life of America--which was so bad for the children of the family, and demoralising for the parents too?"

"No, indeed it is not like hotel life at all! for it is a *home*. This, like most of those, founded by what were then called the middle class, was a proprietary home from the first. Each family has a vested interest in it. My grandmother's second husband was one of the original founders, and he left it to his step-son, Hugh Henderson. I inherited it from my father, as my brother has his occupation in the North of England, and my sister married a man who took her to America. That is an old story, fifty years ago."

"Then did Florrie end her life here?" I asked.

"Yes, certainly she did! Her husband was on a visit to Australia and met her there, and brought her to England in the year 1900, and here he settled till his death."

CHAPTER II

"Then this is really your own property," said I, "to have and to hold, to bequeath or to sell as you please."'

"Not exactly; I can neither bequeath or sell--except to one who would be agreeable to the other dwellers in the home. An upset (sic) price is fixed, and when a vacancy occurs by death or removal, applicants are balloted for."

"It must then be a little difficult for a young couple to settle, unless there are constantly new homes built to be filled?"

"New homes are not often built, for the whole of our present happiness and prosperity depends on the population remaining stationary, and the homes are built so substantially that they will last for hundreds of years if kept in proper repair."

"But what sort of life do you ladies lead without household cares? It looks like all leisure, which I do not think would be either pleasant or useful."

"Oh, by no means all leisure! I have my work to do during the day, and I can either do it here, or in one of the pleasant public rooms down stairs. If I want society I can seek it where it is likely to be most congenial. My own favorite room is the art room; but if I want music I can hear it in the music room; if I want to read I can go to the library, where none of the readers there will disturb me. If I want a game of cards, I can have it in the room dedicated to such quiet games. For the closest intimacy--such as I used to have with my husband in his lifetime, and with my children, and even now with such friends as I wish to talk unreservedly with--as I do with you--I can have this best and sweetest of society here."

"You have then no private sitting room?"

"No, we do not feel the want of it, and it would materially add to the cost of building and keeping up an Associated Home if each family required such a luxury."

"Have you been long a widow?" I asked.

CHAPTER II
26

"My husband died four years ago."

"You are then alone?"

"Oh no! my daughter and her husband and two of their three children live in this home, and shortly there will be another included in the family, for his only daughter is to be married on Thursday, and there have been arrangements made that the young people should live here. Florrie is young, and does not like to leave her mother."

"How many children had you?"

"I had only two who lived. One was born an idiot, owing to a fright I got some months before, and, of course, it was destroyed at birth."

"That is a summary way of disposing of a heavy charge," said I. "In my day there were costly idiot asylums for a few, and idiots in all the workhouses in the kingdom. Why, I saw one in an Australian asylum thirty-four years old, who had never been able to speak, to walk, or to feed herself. I do not know how much longer she lived; but she must have cost the country a large sum."

"It is really the best thing to do to put such imperfect and helpless beings painlessly out of existence." said Mrs. Carmichael calmly. "My other children are quite satisfactory--rather above than below the average. My son is the manager of a large co-operative cotton factory, and he lives with his workpeople during the day, and in an Associated Home near it where his wife's family are established. I see him every Sunday of my life, and occasionally on other days."

"I suppose he lives in a more luxurious way than you do."

"No, I scarcely think so. Of course each home has its little peculiarities and specialties, but the average standard of comfort is about the same."

"As a manager of a large concern he ought to be paid very highly."

"He has invested more capital in the factory than the operatives, and, of course, draws a larger proportion of interest, but for his actual services there is not the difference there would seem to be between direction and actual production. Indeed the tendency is towards equalisation, though that is not reached yet."

"Indeed!" said I, "that is most surprising. Who will you find to take high and difficult positions if there is no adequate payment made?"

"Why, we find people are all eager enough to take the high positions if they are only fit for them. It is far more interesting to direct than to obey. And, after all, people can only eat three meals a day and wear one suit of clothes at a time. What would more money do in adding to one's enjoyment of life?"

"It did much in my time," said I. "Life was cramped and narrowed and harrassed for want of money. Those who had not enough of it for necessaries were starved physically. Those who had a bare livelihood were starved mentally and aesthetically. A sufficient margin of money over and above the supply of material wants meant leisure, amusement, foreign travel, books, pictures, wines; as Charles Lamb would say, 'Money is not dross, it is all these delightful things.' It also allowed us to be hospitable to our friends and charitable to the poor. Cynics and ascetics reviled it, but money was the *open sesame* to much of the beauty and to a great deal of the goodness of life."

"Much that you consider so desirable we obtain now-a-days by means of combination. Much of it appears no longer so attractive as it must have been in the time when 'every gate was barred with gold, and opened but to golden keys,' as my grandmother used to say." I recognised my old Tennyson-lover in the quotation.

"You have then learned to be happy with little money?"

"I do not know what you call little. We feel we have enough. As for leisure, we have no longer what is called a leisured class, but everyone has a great deal of leisure that may be used either for amusement, for self-improvement, for the riding of hobbies, or for what satisfies our modern ideas of charitable work.

CHAPTER II 28

"I suppose you have a general eight-hours system? What a fight there was for that in my time."

"No! Six hours a day is reckoned a day's work in shop or factory. Machinery, which is costly, such as that at my son's cotton factory is worked by relays. There are some occupations and professions in which there can be no such limit; but the general feeling is that six good hours' work for everybody should provide all the necessaries and comforts of life for everybody."

"Then all your people work?"

"With very few exceptions--which count for nothing--every adult man and woman has some bread-earning occupation."

"Married women, too?" I asked.

"Certainly! My daughter, for instance, is a physician, her husband edits a newspaper. Both of them have somewhat irregular hours of labor, but I do not fancy they average much more than six hours daily"

"If the practice is good, and the newspaper has a large circulation they ought to be rich, especially as they have only three children?"

"It is the full number. No one living in an Associated Home is allowed to have more than three children--at least in Europe. I hear that four is allowed in America and Australia."

"Then people ought to become rich with so few demands upon their purses," said I.

"I scarcely know how to express myself." said my kinswoman, "Incomes, I know, were very different in your time. There is a moderate competence within reach of all, but the opportunity of making fortunes is gone. Everywhere co-operation and combination prevents the accumulation of capital in single hands. The professions are not crowded; there are few blanks, but the prizes are not great, and all the great profits which large means used to make for a single capitalist or firm are reduced to a minimum, while each operative gets a share of

CHAPTER II　　　　　　　　　　　　　　　　　　　　　　　　　　　　29

that minimum. As for my daughter's practice, she contracts to watch over the health of the women and children who live in the Owen Home and eight other homes. Sickness is not so costly as it used to be, because in an Associated Home it is one of the items of expense included in the ordinary hoard or contribution made for housekeeping."

"Oh! I see an evolution of the working man's friendly club or lodge, and the homes contract at a cheap rate, no doubt."

"Probably you will think so, especially as the medical adviser is expected to look ahead, and prevent sickness as well as to minister to it. Mrs. Oliphant does a little hospital work too, but that, of course, is gratis."

"And her husband is on the press?"

"He is also a writer of books. He is mainly engaged during his leisure hours in writing a complete history of the co-operative movement. He will thus be the best man for you to consult and enquire from, as he has made it his business to study the beginning of the social system that to us is so old, and to you is so new and strange."

"I have then been most fortunate in the Home to which I have been directed. Not only kinsfolk, but people especially fitted to instruct me in the new *régime*!! So married women as well as single women work for their livelihood now? I could see that change coming even in my day."

"Far more married women than single; for the single life lasts so short a time. Even I am not quite off work yet, I can still earn half of my livelihood, the other half being drawn from my own and my husband's savings, which will last me out, even if I live to a great age."

"What was Mr. Carmichael's avocation?"

"He was an artist. I learned much from him to help me in my own calling of a designer for calico and muslin printing; but I had also a great love for art needlework, and as I am a little old-fashioned for the calico printers I stick to this, and even give lessons in it to the young people."

CHAPTER II   30

"I should have thought there was little demand for painting, and as little for such work as this," and I looked more carefully at the exquisite embroidery which my kinswoman had laid down out of respect for me. "In the flat, dead level of conditions you live in, no one can afford to pay for such commodities."

"There is a limited demand in the Associated Homes and in the Churches. I have had great pleasure in giving a good deal of my work to the Owen Home, as my husband presented to it no less than twelve of his best pictures. We delighted to beautify our home, but I must confess that both my husband's work and mine falls out of demand because everyone has so much leisure, and so many have artistic taste that each home is adorned with work of its own volunteers, but when we began life it was not so."

"The Associated Homes must furnish a market for books also?"

"Yes, our reading rooms or libraries have always a permanent library of standard works. For the modern and ephemeral a syndicate of thirty homes exchange with each other."

"And after running the gauntlet of thirty homes the books are pretty well worn out I suppose?"

"Just so, but the young people, at least, have read them."

"But what about quarrelling? That was the bugbear which threatened all associated living when it was spoken of in my time, for the idea was already in the air a hundred years ago."

"The pioneers had to go through many hard trials. My father told me that during the first ten years there were more changes, resignations and expulsions than there were for fifty years after. The quarrels were sometimes personal, sometimes about children. I am ashamed to say that the women were worse offenders in this way than the men. Now, both men and women have been educated into bearing and forebearing. My grandmother told me that she was within an ace of making her husband sell out, she was so aggravated by the dress and manners and language of the people in the next suite of rooms, but he talked her over, and gradually the people improved."

"Poor Florrie!" said I, "she was a fastidious young personage. Little did she think to end her days as a unit in an Associated Home."

"It took some time, too," said my kinswoman, "to establish the rule that no married couples should have more than three children. They stood out that if they could afford to keep four or five they should not be prevented, and many expulsions followed this infraction. Now it is felt to be as disgraceful to exceed the number, as in old times it was to have a child born out of wedlock."

"That is a curious condition of public opinion."

"It is the keystone of our whole system. Science, too, has put the limitation of the family more completely in our power than when the rule was laid down. People who do not care for children, have none, and some couples who would like them are not blessed with them; so that the limit of three keeps the population stationary."

"I suppose that almost all the children who are born grow to maturity," said I.

"My daughter says that nothing shows the advantages of our social order like the small death rate, and the average long healthy life. The death of infants is very rare indeed, most of the infantile diseases are stamped out. Children do not need now to take measles and whooping-cough any more than they do small-pox. Care is certainly needed during the time of teething, and the changes of weather should be provided against; but our babies are not such tender blossoms as those of our great-grandmothers."

"One would think that so many mothers in a home would quarrel about their children?"

"Well the children are kept in their place, and our nurses are well-educated, good-principled women; but, really, as to quarrelling, the advantages are so enormous in comfort and material well-being, as well as for social intercourse, that people have learned to put their

CHAPTER II
32

pride and their susceptibilities aside. The rules of the home are seldom referred to, but they are tacitly respected by everyone."

"I suppose it has never occurred to you that you would be happier in the old way, the way in which it was last week suggested to me that I should live;--in furnished apartments by myself."

"Certainly not; this is the home I was born in and married in. My widowhood need not sever me from all society."

"Should you not prefer to live with your married daughter and her children in a pleasant house of her own."

"Why I live with her now. I do not bore or restrain her in any way. Old people constantly with two generations of younger ones must have been a tie, and sometimes a nuisance. The younger might also be a nuisance to the old. Elderly people do not like the continual worry of children, who in your old times were very abundant and irrepressible--if I may judge by the light literature of the period."

"I suppose, living in the same house, your daughter devotes herself to you?" said I, recollecting my life with my mother.

"Part of every day she spends with me here. If I am ill, she is my physician, and often my nurse, but her own professional arid public duties carry her outside a great deal. My granddaughter who is a student at the university, and who is to be married to another student on Thursday, always look in on me every day; we meet of course at meals, each family sitting together or opposite, and we see a great deal of each other in the public rooms. But I do not depend altogether on them when I am really ill, as I have been sometimes lately; there are six or seven other people in the house, who have time to spare, and who are glad to bestow it on me."

"The Associated Homes seem to be the paradise of declining years," said I.

"If I feel disposed for society, I can mix with it, and I can choose what group among seven or eight to attach myself to."

"And this without fatigue or expense?" said I. "And as for amusements, I suppose there still exist theatres and concerts, or have you become too utilitarian to care for them, or too poor to pay for the highest talent?"

"We have music and the drama certainly, and the public exhibitions in this way are not costly; but there are entertainments of a similar kind got up in each Associated Home at least twice a week, to which we have the privilege of inviting our friends from outside. This Home, too, is the first that started keeping a carriage for the older and weaker of its members."

"Then the young and healthy do not ride in it?" said I, recollecting the many carriages rolling about everywhere with the healthy wives and daughters of the rich in them, while the old--perhaps infirm--fathers and mothers were supposed to be quite satisfactorily dealt with by being left in the close indoor atmosphere of the fireside.

"Young people can walk and cycle." She used quite a new word; indeed there were many new words in my kinswoman's talk--as might be supposed in a language that had been alive and changing for a hundred years--but I guessed at her meaning by the context. "They can take the public conveyances, but to give old people fresh air and sunshine without fatigue is like life to them."

Our pleasant talk was here interrupted by the penetrating sound of an electric bell. "There is the warning bell for dinner," said she, "it is half-past twelve."

"You call your middle-day meal dinner, and not luncheon?"

"Certainly, because it is dinner."

"What are your hours for meals?"

"Breakfast at half-past seven, dinner at one, and supper at half-past six are our hours at the Owen house."

"People engaged in business cannot all come to a middle-day meal."

CHAPTER II

"Some of the gentlemen engaged in the city take dinner there, but most of us manage to put in an appearance at the chief meal of the day. You will like to take off your bonnet and cloak, and to wash your hands. I shall ring for you to be shown to your room."

"You do not dress for a middle-day dinner, I suppose?"

"Oh, I change this cap, which is good enough for my own room, for a fresher one, and take off my apron; that is all."

"Do you dress for the evening meal, then?"

"The young folks may smarten themselves up a little, but we old folks make no change."

I observed that Mrs. Carmichael's dress showed signs of long service, though it was perfectly neat and spotlessly clean. The material and fashion were both simple and inexpensive.

"I suppose," said I, "that my dress must appear as antidiluvian, as the short-waisted white embroidered dress my mother wore tight before her marriage, and hoarded all her life, appeared to her grand-children."

"No, your dress is rich and most elaborate, but our styles are now as various as our tastes. My own was designed for me by my dear husband when I began to feel I was growing old, and I keep to it. I am having a new dress made for Florrie's wedding, as I needed one, but it is after the old pattern. What is the meaning of that hump at the back? Is it to hide any sort of deformity?"

"By no means. It is to hang the drapery on, and is considered--or was considered--to be indispensable. It helps stout people like myself to have some appearance of a waist."

"What is this rough stuff which sets off the soft woollen material of your dress and mantle? The two blacks are so different from each other."

Had my kinswoman never heard of crape and mourning? "I got the dress nearly a fortnight ago as mourning for my mother; my sister-in-law ordered it for me, and it was rather more costly than I wished or could afford, but Mrs. Grundy--if you ever heard of such a person?"

"I think I have; but I confuse her with the Philistines in some way."

"Mrs. Grundy stands for public opinion, or the opinion of the Philistines, or the least intelligent part of the community. Well, Mrs. Grundy requires mourning to be worn for relatives, and, regardless of ways and means, demands that this mourning should be costly. This crape which is new to you is the authentic and authorised sign of woe; the greater the grief, the nearer the relative in blood to you the deeper should be the crape which is an expensive texture made of silk--though it has none of its lustre. In fact it is a sign of unmitigated woe to be enveloped in crape from head to foot, but, as a shower of rain injures it greatly, that mark of respect is only fit for people who ride in close carriages, or keep indoors."

"I do not wonder at our giving up that practice. Of course I have read of crape in old books, but I have never seen it before."

"Did you not make any alteration in your dress when you became a widow?"

"Certainly not," said Mrs. Carmichael, "I continued to wear the clothes my husband had designed, and that he had seen me in, and that were hallowed by the touch of his dying hands."

"Then you are no slaves to fashion?"

"Fashion, as far as I can gather from the records which I have read, and from the grandmother's talk, was a capricious deity who exacted costly service. We wear such clothes as suit us till they are worn out honestly. We could neither afford to wear such clothes as you have on, or to change them often; but here is Mrs. Cox, ready to show you to your room." "This lady, Mrs. Cox, is my guest for a week; there is a guest-room vacant, I believe?"

CHAPTER II

"Yes, No. 1, which is on this floor," said the attendant, and she led me to a pretty little room, not quite half the size of Mrs. Carmichael's. Everything was on a smaller scale, but in the same style. The bedstead was a single one, and the writing-table with writing materials was half the size of my kinswoman's; there was a cane chair, but no couch, and at the washstand I could have both hot and cold water by turning the taps. I laid aside my outward wrappings, and sat for five minutes at the window to try to take in the situation. I saw from this side of the house, which looked to the back, a garden cultivated in a manner which surpassed all I had seen or dreamed of. Such beds of vegetables--without a weed to be seen in them, such fruit trees on walls and espaliers to catch all they could of the English sun. Golden apricots that reminded me of Australia, downy peaches, rosy apples, melting pears; all the gooseberry and currant tribe were represented, as well as raspberries; strawberries, of course, were over--except for what appeared a late white variety. There must have been ten acres of garden at the back, besides what I had seen from the front. A large shadehouse and a hothouse were placed in the most favourable aspect, so that exotic flowers and fruits might be cultivated as well as the ordinary English varieties. This fruit and vegetable garden appeared to be in charge of three gardeners, who, I saw, put on their coats and go to dinner, probably to their own Associated Homes.

I rose to my feet, shook myself to feel that I was substantially here in the flesh; I looked at myself in the mirror, and I saw that I was the same Emily Bethel who had up to to-day lived and breathed in the atmosphere of the nineteenth century. I took out of my bag the soft cap which I had taken with me for my week's visit and fastened it with the pins provided for guests in No 1 guest-room at the Owen house, which held better than my own. Everything in my bag was as I had packed it. How real and yet so strange was my experience!

My friend was at my door ere I was quite ready, and took me with her down the lift. We walked into the dining-room for adults--to which children were not admitted till they were fourteen years old.

"As a rule the families sit together at meals. I introduce you as an Australian cousin to the community, but you must take Mr. and Mrs. Oliphant into your confidence, as both of them can help you more than

I can to get the full value of your queer bargain." said Mrs. Carmichael. "There, of course, is one frequent guest--soon to be a permanent inmate--Fred. Steele; there is no keeping him away from Florrie."

I was introduced to my kinswoman's daughter, who had a shrewd, sensible face, and a somewhat incisive way of speaking. Mr. Oliphant impressed me even more favorably. Of their two sons, one had settled and married at Liverpool; the other was having his Wanderjahre--his year of travel--before he began his work in his father's newspaper office. His tour was to include America, Africa, and Australia before he returned by India and the Suez Canal.

I therefore could only see one of the younger generation, but I was pleased to see in the seventeen-year-old Florrie of 1988 a great likeness to the Florrie of 1888, especially about the eyes and the turn of the head. After a special study of my relatives, I gave a more comprehensive glance up and down both sides of the table, at which we were seated about the middle, and I felt on the whole very well satisfied with the appearance of the inhabitants of the Owen Home. The expression of restfulness and candour and kindliness which had charmed me with my kinswoman was to be seen on almost every countenance, old and young. Their manners to each other, and to the attendants, were perfect. Matthew Arnold has told us that equality is the best foundation for fine manners, and that the vast disparities in material wealth and in intellectual culture between different classes of society prevent the development of that *respect* humain which is the root of courtesy. I thought of his words as I sat at this dinner table.

As for dress it was on the whole--though various in fashion and style of different ages--much plainer and less expensive than that of middle-class people in my own day. I recollect a newcomer from England asking my mother how people dressed in Adelaide, and she said, curtly, "As well as they can afford to do, and often a great deal better."

As for good looks, I was more than satisfied. The lovely complexion of youth in England was where Florrie and her compeers had the advantage over the Australian ancestors, but the complexion stood even in middle and advanced age, and the physique was altogether

CHAPTER II

finer. Both men and women were taller, larger, and stronger than our old average.

I compared the table, at which about seventy people sat, with one at a *table d'hôte*, or in a large ocean steamer. The appointments were good, though not showy. The tablecloth and table napkins were tolerably fine and beautifully white. Linen, glassware, dinner set, knives, forks and spoons were all marked Owen Home, and could be replaced when worn out or broken. The twenty middle-class families of the nineteenth century would each have had at least two sets of china, stoneware and glass, and of the more expensive an extra number for purposes of hospitality. Thus there was a large saving made in the original outlay and maintenance for the twenty families. The food was abundant and excellently cooked and served, but there was far less meat on the table than I was accustomed to see. Three of the families were absolutely vegetarians, but, independent of that, vegetable diet took a much greater place in the food of the people now that all classes lived alike, and when England was expected to provide for her own population. Soups made largely from pulses, a profusion of vegetables--some familiar to me, but others quite new, salads, light puddings and pastry, and a large quantity of fruit--raw and cooked, with white and brown bread *à discretion* made up the dinner, which I enjoyed very much. There was a large profusion of water drinkers, but some drank light beer or wine with dinner. I was told that those paid a little more, and the vegetarians a little less, as their contribution for housekeeping than the average rate. Four expert waiters--two men and two women--waited at the table. The children had had their dinner half-an-hour earlier in their own dining-room. The meal lasted about forty minutes or three-quarters of an hour, and was enlivened with talk--chiefly amongst the separate families, but occasionally more general. I was interested in some talk about the prospects of the next Presidential election between some opposite neighbors, and I could not help watching with interest the boy and girl, the student lovers who were at my side.

Mrs. Oliphant went after dinner to visit some patients in a Home, Hounslow way. The lovers went for a walk preparatory to settling down to their afternoon work.

Mr. Oliphant--whom I took at once into my confidence--had five leisure hours before going to his office, which he was accustomed to spend either in the library for the preparation of his book on "Co-operation," or in the garden--for he was an enthusiastic horticulturalist; but he was too interested in my story to do anything but devote himself to me. My accurate information and shrewdness up to a certain date, my ignorance and helplessness about all subsequent matters gradually convinced him that I was a belated fellow mortal astray in another century.

Mr. Oliphant was at this particular time a member of the house committee of the Owen Home, and he showed me all over it. First we went to the kitchen--with its marvellous cooking range, and the central fire which warmed sufficiently the whole building at a very small cost for each family even in winter. The same economy characterised the lighting of the establishment by the electric light. The drainage was perfect, and the consequence was that the health of the little community was generally excellent.

Supplies were procured from co-operative stores, which again were connected with cooperative farms and factories. All the processes of production, distribution and consumption were made inter-dependent, and while the cost of production and the labor employed in getting the product to the consumer were minimised, everyone had a share in the profit. It was difficult to compare prices with ours. Perhaps the bushel of wheat was the nearest to accuracy. I could see that a man's work for the day of six hours might be reckoned at the price of a bushel-and-a-half of wheat, and a woman's at a bushel-and-a-quarter. The relation which a bushel of wheat bore to other commodities was, however so different from what I was used to that this unit is somewhat misleading. Prices were marvellously steady, but on the whole the day's work tended to procure more of the necessaries and comforts of life every decade. Wheat was grown in England for the bulk of its supplies, but other cereals and pulses took a large place in cultivation, while the minor industries--too much neglected on large capitalist farms--were developed to the utmost extent on the large co-operative farms which had taken their place; the dairy, pigs and poultry, and fruit and vegetable productions for consumption enormously increased. The Owen Home grew all its own fruit and vegetables, and supplied

CHAPTER II

itself with honey from the garden. The waste from the garden and the house fed the pigs and poultry, but milk was bought, and dairy produce as well as bread, meat, general groceries and beer and wine from the co-operative stores with which the Home was affiliated. The twenty families, without servants, numbered 104 old and young; for though the number of children was limited, it was so much the custom for two or three generations to inhabit the same home that there was more than the old average of five.

I went through the public rooms, each set apart for its specific purpose, and I noted how the hands of various members during three generations had beautified and enriched the common property. I saw, too, how furniture--originally well made--would last if properly cared for and not cast aside for fashion's sake. When the Home was founded in 1900 each member was supposed to put in so much money for the purchase and the furnishing. In order to economise the cost, most of the associates contributed out of their old abandoned homes some things that would take the place of new. Mrs. Carmichael's bedroom furniture was still in great part what Florrie and her husband had put into it. There were still chairs and tables in the whist room and the smoking room, and others, which dated as far back, and the best violins in the music room, as well as one piano, were as old. The mechanics' room was not only utilised for all repairs, which were made properly and efficiently, but many pieces of furniture--such as easy chairs, couches and occasional tables--were made there with the latest improvements in comfort and economy. I saw and admired Mr. Carmichael's paintings, and his widow's needlework.

There was nothing of the meretricious and showy decorations of the present hotel or fashionable boarding house in the appointments and decorations of the Associated Home. Though inhabited by as many families as would make a hamlet or small village the place looked and felt like a home, and I could see that each member felt an owner's pride in it. Inside I could see traces of this everywhere, and there were quite a dozen of the families who had a taste for gardening, and worked at the flower beds and greenhouses--and even at the kitchen garden in their leisure hours.

CHAPTER II
41

There was a committee for floral decorations, who arranged them in the public rooms before breakfast each day. There was also an amusement committee who arranged and carried out the programmes of the Owen Home entertainments, week by week. When Mr. Oliphant took me round the garden--which was his own special health-giving hobby, he showed me more in detail that minute and extensive cultivation which was the rule in the England of the 20th century, and dwelt upon the fact that, by the larger and more varied use of fruit and vegetables as diet, the race had improved in health, and, besides, the land had been able to support in plenty a population which must have emigrated elsewhere, or been insufficiently nourished when English manufactures no longer supplied the rest of the world.

"To-morrow you must see agriculture proper, where the same principle is carried out to waste nothing, and to coax mother earth to produce her uttermost. You must also see the factory system. That will be enough for one day. This day, it should suffice to make yourself acquainted with the machinery of our Associated Homes, the unit in our society, from which commercial associations proceeded, rising to national association up to the confederation of the world for peaceful industry and interchange of commodities and ideas."

"But you say that the export trade of England has departed:"

"In the gigantic form which it used to rear, it is no more; but there are still some foreign goods we must buy and we must export an equivalent. Although foreigners and colonists no longer depend on the capital, labor, and ingenuity of England for their manufactured goods, but supply themselves, there are still some lines which force their way into the markets of the world, because they are better and, for the quality, cheaper than the home product, and this, sometimes in the face of a protective tariff. For instance, Australia cannot manufacture cottons to compete with us, and we share that large market with the United States. In iron goods, America, perhaps, exports more value than we do--but we hold our own. There is a limited demand in the more backward East for some of the comforts and conveniences of life. On the whole we export what procures us what we need from abroad, and thus make life richer and pleasanter for ourselves and others."

CHAPTER II

"I must make the most of my week:" I said, "but there is so much to see and to learn that it seems all too short."

The evening meal was announced before I could take in all I wanted to do of the Associated Home and its working. Supper, as it was called, was different from the dinner, because there was no meat or even fish upon the table. There was tea, coffee and cocoa, and a quite new beverage--patronised by the vegetarians--bread, butter, preserves, light puddings, salads, and an abundance of fruit. Meat was only eaten once a day--even by those who were not vegetarians, but the best vegetable substitutes in the way of pulses were largely consumed, especially at breakfast, which I was told was a more substantial meal than supper. Wheaten and oaten porridge and lentils or other legumes were eaten at breakfast, with eggs prepared in various ways, bacon and fish. I never ate more delicious bread and butter in my life than at supper--the only recollection that came at all near to it was at Paris. Three meals a day made the regular course. Invalids might have food more frequently, but healthy children and adults were supposed to be abundantly nourished with breakfast, dinner, and supper. I contrasted the meals with those of the Melbourne well-to-do, and found that though different they were substantially as good; but, when I contrasted them with those of the Australian working men with meat and tea and bread three times a day, I could see that the working men of the future had a far more healthy dietary, and as for the children at whom I had a peep, there was no comparison.

After supper Mr. Oliphant went to his office, but for me and all others there was an evening, and my kinsfolk asked me where I should like to spend it. I saw by the programme that there was a little dramatic entertainment in which Florrie Oliphant and her lover were to take part, so I chose to go there. The half hour before the performance began I spent in looking through the public rooms and seeing how affinities grouped themselves. I also had a peep at the younger children being put to bed, but I must delay my remarks on the children until I can embrace the whole subject.

The acting was quiet, but very pleasing and remarkably equal. I never heard the prompter at all. Florrie reminded me even more of her great great grandmother in the slight alteration of dress than before, but there was very little make-up in the little play. The piece was so very different in plot from what I was used to--and even in character--that I did not quite know whether I liked it or not, but I knew quite well that I liked the acting.

When I went up to my room, I took pen in hand, and sat down to the little writing-table to commit to paper the wonderful events and experiences of the day. This took so long a time and excited me so much that it must have been far in the morning before I dropped off to sleep. The morning bell awoke me before I had had half enough of the refreshing oblivion of sleep--of deep, dreamless sleep; but I did not ask for a week in the future to waste it in over much slumber. I rose briskly, plunged into a cold bath--and felt a new woman--put on my clothes with a somewhat uncomfortable feeling of being over-dressed for the morning in the Owen Home, and hastened down to eat with excellent appetite a well served and delicious breakfast.

CHAPTER III

TUESDAY

Co-operative Production and Distribution

Mr. Oliphant kindly put himself at my disposal for the day; as he did his six hours' work and more during the night, his days were unoccupied except by the two hobbies of literature and gardening. He felt that my coming would throw light on the subject of his new book, as it showed how different society was in the infancy of co-operation, so that no hobby was equal to the pleasure of enlightening me, who could not stay to read his book. If I did not get whole chapters fired off to me, I feel sure that I had a great many detached sentences. The newspaper seemed to be a very inadequate vehicle for such a man to express himself in. There did not seem to be the same anxiety for the latest news that had characterised the world when I knew it well. I was surprised to see the small size of the paper which my friend edited, and especially the handful of advertisements which appeared in it. I thought this must be a journal with small circulation, or recently established, but in this I was mistaken. The title was the *Daily News*, and it was the present representative of that old Liberal paper.

"What has become of the advertisements?" said I.

"Well, people do not advertise much now-a-days. When the whole community deal at co-operative stores, they need neither showy buildings nor insinuating shopmen nor costly advertisements. The stores do not overstock themselves, and therefore do not need to push their trade!"

"The advertisements used to be the very sinews of war!"

"Yes, indeed; the tail grew so strong that it wagged the head. We still are a good deal beholden to our advertisements, though you look on them with scorn!"

"You see a column or two of vacancies in Associated Homes, and at this season a large number offered at the seaside, for occasional change of air is good for everyone, though not so necessary now that we understand sanitation. Here is a column of Lost and Found, another for situations wanted, and for persons to fill situations. A column of shipping advertisements and a few auction sales of cargoes, which in a general way are consigned to special importers and are not put up to auction, some notices of removal. Births, marriages, divorces, and deaths of course take the first place on the first page!"

"Divorces?" I said.

"Yes; they are public matters, deserving of brief official announcement, though not of exhaustive and exhausting reports as in old times!"

"But where are the quack medicines and the toilet requisites? Where are Holloway's Pills, Eno's Fruit Salt, Pears' Soap, Hop Bitters, and such like?"

"Not now worth advertising apparently. Sales are made to the stores, which are not induced to buy by plausible advertisements!"

"Where are the new season's goods just opened,--where the tremendous sacrifices of goods at the end of the Summer and Winter seasons, and the detailed price-list to tempt the lover of bargains?"

"Gone for ever, I suppose, because our co-operative stores do not over-buy in the first place, and neither charge a fancy price for what is novel, nor reduce below cost when the article has become common or has induced cheaper imitations. We keep our wares till the next season, we wear out our own clothes and consume or work up our own scraps; but with the death of the fury of competition fell the enormous profits of newspapers on advertisements which enabled them to spend what appears to us now fabulous sums for the latest news. I can see that you look on our modern *Daily News* as a very poor affair, but you may see that other journals are in the same category."

There were five other daily papers and six weekly taken in at the Owen Home, but all had the same characteristics. The *Times* was larger than the *Daily News*, and had more foreign intelligence, but no larger advertising sheets.

I was indeed surprised. "It is not only the new goods and the season sales that I miss, but the sales of real estate, of stock, of shares."

"I suppose there is a character of permanence in all our doings that was unknown to you. A family goes into a home, and, as you see, remains there for life, and often for generations. A farm or a factory, on co-operative principles, helps its employés together, not by the week or the month, but for the life-time. Exchanges are sometimes made, but it is advantageous to keep together, and the element in human nature that leads to constancy is encouraged by all our social arrangements. But this permanence is not the thing to make newspapers either so interesting to read, or so lucrative to manage as when people could be tempted to almost any course of action by having it forcibly presented to them."

"Personally, I hated the advertising system. I do not think I ever bought anything in consequence of having it presented insistently; but I must have been an exception, or the thing could not have been kept up," said I.

"You see that we do not get as much for a penny as you used to do. The advertisements are fewer and cheaper. Twenty families associated do not buy so many newspapers. We pay the employés as much or more in value for six hours' work as was formerly paid for ten, and the price of paper would have been raised by the high value of labor if cheaper fibre had not been discovered, and more effective machinery applied to the manufacture."

"It is indeed a strange industrial revolution that has been carried out. Our prevalent idea was that things would continue to go on expanding, and that the 20th century would go into bigger figures in every way than the 19th, but with you the general well-being of the whole population demands checks somewhere, and I see it in the newspaper clearly enough The cost of advertising enhances the cost of the product, and your whole system demands the minimising of the cost of distribution, so that the producer should get as much and the consumer pay as little as possible."

CHAPTER III

"You put the case in a nutshell," said Mr. Oliphant."

"But what do the armies of distributors do, not to speak of the speculators, the brokers, and stock jobbers. Of actual producers every country showed too few, and yet they appeared to produce too much for the consumers to buy at a remunerative price. The fringe of casual workers taken on at a push, and cast off in slack seasons, showed something very far from sound in the industrial world, and scarcely less objectionable was the fury of overwork alternated with none at all in many of the season trades. Painters and decorators, for instance, were over-driven for six months in the year, and half idle for the other six."

"Our social system now," said Mr. Oliphant, "is built on the continuous employment of all the population. Painters and decorators, as you say, are still living during the summer at this branch of their business, but they are employed in making paper hangings and other material that will keep during the winter months. Every one has a by-trade, which may be scarcely as profitable as his ordinary one, but the misery and waste of enforced idlenesss is saved to him. This needs organisation and management, which you will see to advantage at our co-operative farm."

"How far is it out of London?" I asked.

"About forty miles. My brother is the manager, and will be glad to show a stranger from Australia over the place. You will travel by a national railway."

"That I was used to; in all the colonies railways were built and controlled by the Government. How did the nation absorb the iron roads built by associations of capitalists?" "Not by spoliation--the nation gave the full value to the companies for them." "Is travelling cheapened in consequence?"

"Yes, considerably cheapened, and made much more safe as well."

"I cannot comprehend how, in a century, the great disparities of condition have been virtually abolished, and the nation seems in the process to have exchanged national debt for national property. You have no rich people now-a-days."

"Yes, we have some whom we call rich, but the very rich are extinct."

"You must have confiscated property on a large scale. It may have been necessary, but it must often have been very cruel."

"It was not confiscation, as I understand the word," said Mr. Oliphant, "but something had to be done when the armies of Europe were disbanded, and the millions of non-producers, who had simply destroyed capital and consumed the fruits of others' toil, must needs be enlisted in the industrial army. All trades stood aghast at the threatened competition. In old thickly-peopled countries it was not as in America at the close of her civil war, when an enormous area of fertile land was open for new settlement, and Europe ready to buy the produce of labor, and besides, there the armies had been improvised recently out of industrious citizens. The European standing armies were composed of soldiers untrained to peaceful labor. The Continental armies were larger than the English, no doubt, but their land system was better. It was not the mere soldiers who had to be provided for, but there were thousands on thousands of artisans engaged from their youth up in making rifles, cannons, and all the munitions of war by sea and land, thrown at once out of employment. The land system had to be revolutionised, and all of the land utilised. Then was the tremendous stride taken in co-operative production, and the simultaneous exchange of the isolated for the Associated Homes. It was a terrible but a grand time to live in. In the peaceful serenity of our present days, I have often sighed for the opportunities of that time of transition. The wisdom and philanthropy of the best of the educated classes were called out as they have never been before or since, organising workshops and trade instruction, and especially in revolutionising agriculture."

"Was it peasant properties or *petite culture* that they went in for, or long leases with compensation for improvements?"

"Not small peasant properties; modern agriculture to be successful, must be carried on on a large scale, with every appliance in the way of machinery, and the most effective division of labor that can be accomplished. It was an age when the capital which had been gradually earning less and less in the old channels, was poured out on the land like water; when new fertilisers, some bulky and others minute, were tried and tested all over the country from Land's End to John O'Groat's, and when for the first time, the body of the people understood the population question."

"The nation would of course save the enormous cost of the army and navy." said I, "but in such a crisis the taxes would fall off, and would be remitted."

"No, the taxes were not remitted. They were very severe, but the nation used this money and the credit which still stood good, for all other countries were passing through an equally difficult crisis, to buy up encumbered estates. All crown lands, church lands, and waste lands are at once nationalised, and let with absolute fixity of tenure for a rent or land tax, call it what you will. The waste lands blossomed like the rose, and the non-producers became producers of wealth not before dreamed of."

"We thought British farming was very advanced."

"I have the statistics at the office, which would surprise you. The average product in food of various kinds to the acre is very much more than when the land was cultivated by capitalist tenant farmers employing hired labor."

"But the nation has not bought up all the land in what I gather from conversation you now call the Commonwealth of Great Britain and Ireland."

"By no means, but all other estates are dealt with by their owners in the same way. Many estates were so encumbered that it was impossible for the owners to hold them longer, and they were divided and sold to co-operative companies in blocks for farming. All entails and hindrances to sale of land were done away with, so that the great land-owner is a tradition of the past. Land kept up its value long because the possession of it gave a social position which other property could not do, but with the collapse of foreign trade, and the

CHAPTER III 50

competition of foreign and colonial manufactures, the large fortunes were no longer made that sought for this Hall-mark of gentility."

"And what of the wheat growers of America, Australia, and India, not to speak of Russia, who used to supply your industrious producers of manufactured articles with cheap bread? Their occupation would be gone."

"There was, as I have told you, a terrible period all over the world. You must have seen the beginning of the industrial revolution, when the foreigners and colonists began to shake off the yoke of dependence on Britain. This continued till the unemployed in England were counted by millions; Capitalists stood aghast at the gradually waning profits of all industrial undertakings, which turned indeed to a steady loss, and were glad for years to live on their capital without looking for interest at all. Then as I said, the preventive population check was adopted not only by the middle class, but by artisans and laborers, and there was an emigration for (sic) England which rivalled that from Ireland after the famine. Australia received a large contingent during the ten years at the close of the last century, and at the beginning of this, which she absorbed advantageously in settling her vast territory. America, as might be expected, received a still larger access of people. The cheapness of transport caused a large number to go to Canada, than to your more distant settlement. But Australasia, as might be expected now far outnumbers Canada in population."

"But other European countries would be equally embarrassed with over-population."

"All these countries sent large bodies of emigrants to North and South America, and to Australasia, but England was the country *par excellence* which had a large proportion of the people absolutely dependent on foreign trade and foreign food."

"The great Republic grew rich on the emigration of Europe. Has that exodus now ceased?"

"The great Republic, like other nations, has learned how to be self-contained and self-supporting. The millionaires who had been made rich in the mechanical inventions supplied to an intelligent people who had abundance of land to fall back upon, and especially by the railroads, which conveyed the produce to the sea-board, suffered in the collapse of the export trade. Their railways became less profitable, and were nationalised sooner than ours. America, after a period of great expansion, has settled down to a stationary population of about one hundred and fifty millions"

"And Australia?" I asked eagerly.

"Australasia including New Zealand, has now a population of fifty millions, and is capable of much expansion yet."

"The United Kingdom or Commonwealth, as you call it, can no longer maintain as its own territory the thirty-five millions of a century back--of my yesterday."

"No, it fell through emigration, and the preventive check, to thirty millions, and keeps stationary at that."

"This does not look like progress," I said. "All our ideas of prosperity were connected with an increasing population."

"In a new country like yours, population was wealth--the more hands you could enlist in developing your soil, and your vast resources, the more general was the well being, but a limit is found at length. Of the thirty millions who now people England and Wales, Scotland and Ireland, all are living in comfort; there are no longer a third of the community existing in the borderland of starvation. Pauperism has died out, so that heavy drain on the industry of the people has been removed, as well as the cost of war, and of the fear of war, which was worse than the conflict itself. You will find also as you become acquainted with our social system, that many of the things which were established at great cost and which were a continuous tax on productive industry, are carried out by armies of volunteers in their leisure, which every one has so large a share of."

"How do you employ all your thirty millions of people. It does not need so many to produce food and clothing, and moderate necessaries for

CHAPTER III 52

home consumption."

"You forget that each producer is a large consumer. That a well-to-do working class (to use the old phrase,) which is well and plainly fed, comfortably clothed and lodged, well educated, and well amused, makes a large market for all sorts of commodities. A market steady and quite unaffected by the changes of fashion."

"It was held that without the lavish expenditure of the rich, the artisan and factory hand could not earn a living," said I, "but I always combated that idea."

"What is the market created by one rich man waited on by say twenty unproductive servants, compared to that of two hundred producers, fed and clothed and lodged as we are in our Associated Homes, with the minimum of labor required to wait on us, and set us free for our various bread-earning avocations?" said Mr. Oliphant.

"The wealth of the past certainly was accompanied by enormous waste, and was confronted and overbalanced by enormous want, but people justified the lavish expenditure of the rich on the ground that it employed labor, which was always super-abundant, and always ready to flow in any direction which their tastes or caprice opened. Whether in the form of a hundred guineas for a ball-dress, or a thousand pounds for the floral decorations at a single entertainment, this circulation of money was held to enrich the producing classes."

"How much of it stuck to the fingers of the middlemen? Are not the dressmakers who make our wives' and our daughters' simple clothes better paid and better treated than the fabricators of hundred guinea marvels, and is it not better that flowers should be a part of our daily life and seen in abundance in the homes of all the community, than that costly exotics should be grown for the demand of millionaires? Thank God we have done with millionaires. They had their uses in the production of capital which stimulated invention, but they were the most demoralising of consumers."

"I suppose more people are employed in the land than formerly. In my time great complaints were made that machinery entered into farming

CHAPTER III 53

so much that agricultural laborers were at a discount, and the best of the country people crowded into the towns or emigrated to the colonies, leaving the old and feeble and the paupers a burden on the community."

"We employ far more machinery than ever, but we also employ more manual labor. The great decline is in the factory hands as the foreign trade is so small now, but machinery and inventions had not said their last word even in your time, and we must export, not only to pay for the raw material of other countries, such as cotton and silk, but for those articles of food which we desire which we cannot grow in this climate."

"Tea, coffee, wine, sugar?"

"We do not import much sugar. Much of our soil is admirably fitted for beet."

"And the sugar-growers in the West Indies and in Queensland are cut out of their market." I remonstrated.

"We still draw some sugar from the West Indies, but these islands have learned to vary their industries. As for Queensland and Palmerston they supply Australasia with cane sugar, which is better liked than beet, and as there is a fiscal union over all the colonies, they have the command of the market."

"Would it not be cheaper and in every way better for England to import cane sugar and other things which are not suited to her climate, than to fight with nature to produce them?" said I, for I had been reared in the orthodox doctrine of political economy, and I thought that to draw our daily supplies from the farthest corners of the earth was not only magnificent but economical.

"I cannot undertake to answer that question. Society has come to the conclusion that whether the articles cost more or not, it is better to pay a little higher price and be more independent of the outside world. The hostile tariffs that the undutiful daughters of Great Britain one after another erected as barriers against the products and manufactures of the mother country, were probably an economical mistake for a time,

CHAPTER III

and were somewhat blindly entered into, but I believe it was thus that the world struggled into the knowledge that the *nearest* market is, on the whole, the *most profitable*, and that the well-being and the varied efficiency of our own producers are the chief things to be considered."

"Now that you have established a certain standard of living, a certain limitation of labor, and a certain rate of wages, you will be forced to keep out foreign competition."

"We are," said Mr. Oliphant. "Fancy coolies and Chinese coming to destroy all we have struggled for! But this does not need legislation. Public opinion makes it difficult if not impossible for a stranger to find employment."

"It is like a mighty trade union," said I. "There was great exception taken to many of the exclusive ideas and unjustifiable methods of the trade associations in my time, but there is no doubt they did a great deal of good."

"They occupied the transition ground between individualism and collectivism. The interests of the single workman were lost in that of his trade, but at first the union had no feeling for the vast mass of inorganised labor, which had no such protection from encroachment, and they actually made the position of these, including all female workers, more intolerable. Now we feel all members of one body, and there is no avocation, however humble, that serves society, that is not respected and adequately paid for."

"But if you keep out cheap labor, you must also keep out the products of the cheaper labor of other countries."

"The continental countries have all established systems similar to ours, for they were ahead of us in the social revolution. The well-being of the workman is measured by the fertility of the soil and the pressure of population, and in a smaller degree by the capital that has been accumulated to develop industries."

"I should also say by the intelligence of the people." said I.

"France took the lead in seeing the necessity of a stationary population," said Mr. Oliphant. "Germany, when she worked up to the situation, and had no longer the drain of her armies, which took from every citizen five years of productive life, besides the cost of the permanent force and artillery and fortifications, excelled France in the thoroughness of her social reforms. Her soil is not so rich as that of England or France, but the industry of her people is marvellous. In Germany they work eight hours a day still. In France and Italy and Spain only seven hours."

"What are the hours in America and Australia?"

"Six hours, but I believe the style of living is more luxurious than here."

"And Russia," said I eagerly, "Has Russia obtained freedom?"

"Oh yes, long ago. It is strange to look back a hundred years. Russia is still backward as compared to England, but there was a marvellous movement after the fall of the Autocracy. You had the French Revolution as your type of terrible catastrophe: that was nothing to the Russian Revolution. Hard as was our task in reconstruction, the settlement of Russia was harder, and there were many noble souls released from years of prison and exile, who plunged into the work and spent themselves for their weaker and more ignorant brethren. Russia has great, indeed immense resources. Like America, she has every variety of soil and climate (outside of the tropical), and enlightened agriculture has done marvels for her, though the want of a middle class was a great hindrance for her for a whole generation. I may say for nearly two generations."

"What heavy protective tariffs you must have to keep out foreign products."

"Foreign products are not now so much cheaper than our own. With regard to Europe and America and Australia, freight and charges are almost sufficient protection. It is a matter of time with regard to the Eastern or Asiatic commodities."

"India, China, and Japan--at least if the workman there continues to subsist on a handful of rice--must be able to undersell your highly paid European cultivator and artisans."

"They have not the aid of machinery, and invention, and effective association of labor to any great extent yet, though they have made a beginning; but as for the bare margin of subsistence they are learning from the West to demand more, and, as the first step towards this, they now limit their population."

"The religion of India, and that of China also, favored the reckless multiplication of the species."

"What known religion of any antiquity did not," said Mr. Oliphant, "except the ascetic form of medieval Christianity, which encouraged celibacy among the most gracious and intelligent of the population, and left the race to be perpetuated by the ignorant and violent. Every church and creed and priesthood in the world fought to the death against the prudential check, but religion is forced to give way, or to accept modifications when its requirements are felt to be destructive or subversive of happiness and progress. Female infants were always ruthlessly murdered in China, but male infants were prized because they alone could perform the necessary rites on the death of a parent. It is now found that the nearest male relative can do this as well, and the proportion of quite childless couples is even greater in China than in India. The population of both vast territories has steadily decreased for the last seventy years, and the well-being of the inhabitants has advanced in a similar degree."

"Of course England no longer possesses her splendid Indian Empire."

"No! But she has the glory of having prepared this vast dependency for self-government--not as one empire, but as a confederacy of states. Their institutions are not closely modelled on ours, but are suited to the genius and to the circumstances of these people."

"The British Islands have a great history." I said. "Mother of nations planted by all waters, and, in India, the administrator and educator of a foreign empire. It must have seemed hard to give up the vast prestige

CHAPTER III   57

and power of a Colonial and Indian Empire, and to have settled down to the position--held before the days of Chatham--of a small European group of islands, living on its means. Where are the openings now for enterprising young men? It is difficult for me to conceive of a state of society where different members of families were not scattered abroad. With my own limited family connections I had relatives in Scotland, London, Victoria, New Zealand, South Australia, Canada, Canary, the West Indies, the United States, Ceylon, and India, China and Fiji--not to speak of others in houses of business trading with these and other distant parts. It appears a sad come down for Imperial Britain."

"As in the case of our ordinary families, the children have become independent. They still love their parent State, and honor her; but they do not depend on her. She, too, has made herself independent."

"What then are your chief industries?"

"Agriculture and horticulture; but, of course, there are still great factories for the production of everything but the raw material. The six hours' labor daily is aided by all the machinery and appliances which the feverish age of competition, in which you have lived, gave birth to for the advantage in the race of wealthy individuals. That age, indeed, was mainly employed in equipping civilised man with economic tools to use in a quieter and happier social order. Had the reconstruction of the industrial world taken place a hundred years--or even fifty years earlier--the unit of production would have been much less. Material well-being would have been lower in degree, and procured with more labor."

"I recollect the socialists and anarchists said that four hours' labor daily would suffice for the wants of the world."

"We prefer six, and go beyond necessaries to comforts: but now we reap the full advantage of the conquering machine."

"Your short day's work is wasteful for costly machinery."

"No! Such machinery is worked in shifts--as many as three shifts in the cotton and woollen factories, and in some of the ironworks. Two shifts,

CHAPTER III 58

daily, in all factories. The only direction in which longer hours of work are occasionally allowed is in agriculture. At haymaking and harvest time all hands will work double tide (sic), if necessary."

"They do not now call in extra hands to help, as was the custom when I knew the world."

"What could these extra hands do for the rest of the year? Our industrial system is built upon permanent, and continuous employment. The terrible evils of out-of-workness, or, as the French concisely termed it, *chomage*, rose to such a height at the latter end of the nineteenth century that it caused starvation in many cases, imperfect nutrition for millions, put a strain upon charity and philanthropy under which they collapsed, and threatened revolution and anarchy."

"You *had* a revolution. It was not merely threatened."

"Yes! But not such as that of France in the 18th century, or of Russia in the 19th. It was not anarchic but reconstructive. However, such as it was, *chomage* was its most dangerous element, and the thing had to be put an end to, at whatever cost."

"I recollect, indeed, the foolish speech of a fashionable lady who had delayed giving the order for her dress in the London season till the last moment, and the dressmaker said it could not be done. 'Why not put on fresh hands?"

"That meant," said Mr. Oliphant, "that outside of the regular workers there should be a contingent to suit the caprices of employers, and to be cast off to starve at other times."

"There is far too much of that in all season trades, I fear," said I. *Chomage* was one of the things that weighed heavy on my mind in the last fifteen years of my life. But six hours seems an absurdly short day. I recollect the alarm at the shortening of hours lest it should destroy England's supremacy as against the cheaper labor and longer hours of continental producers. Six hours cannot be universal. The attendants at your Homes must be on duty much longer."

CHAPTER III 59

"Yes! But not at the stretch, all the time, like an operative in a factory or workshop."

"I used to think shopmen in England, and especially barmen and barmaids were kept on the stretch for very long days and domestic service where employers were not considerate was not much better. On the go from early morn till long past dewy eve."

"Our people relieve each other a good deal in the homes. Our work is done by contract, and there is perfect organisation amongst the attendants. There is no complaint of overwork. We have had the same staff substantially for ten years, as the contract is renewed yearly."

"Your attendants do so much," said I, "compared with service as I recollect it."

"Machinery lightens the work in every direction: knives and boots and silver are cleaned by machinery; there are no fires to light or grates to clean; sweeping is done in an ingenious method which you never heard of, which raises no dust: nothing could give less trouble than the lighting of the Owen Home. You saw the cooking apparatus, the boilers, roasters, and steamers, the peelers, shellers, and choppers, which are so useful when food has to be prepared in quantity, but which are not worth buying for every isolated home. It is the same in every department. I feel certain that except in the textile arts, six hours' work is as effective now as ten when you left the world."

"The personal service must be much more effective," said I, "unless your twenty families need far less waiting on than their ancestors."

"Probably they do. They do not ring the bell and bring a domestic up two flights of stairs to tell what is wanted, and send her down for it. Even with the lift, and the telephone, our attendants have little of that kind of interruption. All necessary orderly services in the way of cleaning the house, cooking, and serving the meals, and washing and getting up clothes, are given to us without our having the trouble of ordering it."

CHAPTER III

"Then you are never put out because the cook has gone off in a huff on the eve of a large dinner party, or the girl who minds the baby leaves on short notice for an easier place."

"You observe that we call our attendants Mr., Mrs., or Miss as the case may be. We respect them, and save them by machinery from much disagreeable labor. We plan all we can to economise unproductive human labor."

"And productive human labor also," said I, "because the more each worker can turn out the better for the consumer.'"

"Quite true; but a reduction in the number of those who give personal service to others for their livelihood is one of the most remarkable features in our civilisation. It began in a faint and tentative way before the industrial revolution."

"I recollect going into some statistics in Victoria, where domestic servants were more highly paid, and had more privileges than anywhere in the world, and I noticed that while in ten years the general population had increased so that there were twenty thousand more inhabited houses, the number of female domestic servants had only increased by three hundred. Our newspapers laid the blame of this on protected industries, which attracted the girls to factories and shops, but I could not see that so many of them went there. A large proportion seemed to prefer to stay at home."

"It was the objection to the conditions of service that was at work everywhere."

"The objection told hard on the mothers of young families who were not rich. They could not get help for love or money."

"That pressure affected society in two ways," says Mr. Oliphant. "It tended to limit the number of children to what the mother herself could attend to, and to substitute for the old service the present independent contract, which is best carried out in associated homes.'"

This, I think, was the substance of our conversation on the railway carriage, which took us in a little over an hour to the co-operative farm, forty miles out of London, northward, which was managed by Mr. George Oliphant. It was a busy time of the year, all hands were out in the harvest-field, which, however, was so near the house that they were able to come in for middle-day dinner, so that I could see the agricultural laborer of the twentieth century at his work and at his meal. Reaping machines were used, not worked by horses. In the matter of horses, the age was most economical. Some of these machines were worked by cable like the tramways, but those on this co-operative farm of Ossulton were worked by pneumatic pressure by steam, but with a saving of fuel such as I had never heard of. That also was the case with the railway on which I had travelled. The wheat harvest was in full swing, and the day was hot. The produce, I was told, was equal to fifty bushels to the acre, but the reckoning was in centals, and indeed decimal coinage and decimal weights and measures had been adopted so long ago that most people had forgotten our old standard. The farm measured about 5,000 acres, mostly gently undulating country, but there was something like a hill which had been cut in terraces by a steam scoop, and which took its turn in the rotation of crops. The proportion of stock kept to the arable was smaller than of yore, because new and less bulky manures supplanted in part the old farm-yard compost, which was also made the most of. Great pits of ensilage was stored, as well as turnips and mangolds, for winter consumption for sheep and cattle. The minor industries were legion, as well as what may be called outside crops. There was beet, and flax and hemp, rye and a hardy millet. A choice plot was planted with hops, which were not now confined to Kent. There were fields of peas and beans, not exclusively for horses' food as of old. The well-being of the community was greatly aided by the utilisation of old despised products for human food. Vegetables were grown for sale, as well as to supply plentifully all the hands employed on the farm. Fruit trees were planted for shelter where I had been used to see belts of firs or other forest trees. Now that the building trades had collapsed, and shipbuilding had also died out, for the needs of the world were served by swift iron steamers mostly, there was a very limited market for building timber, and so the food-producing apple, pear, plum, and nut trees were substituted. A large dairy farm employed continuously several of the inhabitants of Ossulton House. Another contingent had charge of the pigs and the poultry, which were kept in far larger proportions than in the old capitalist farms. Poultry farming has, indeed, grown to a scientific pursuit, and it was quite possible for every citizen to have a fowl in the pot on Sundays, according to the kindly but ineffectual wish of *Henri Quatre*. The very bee-hives of the farm aided in the common fund considerably. No more eggs, butter, or cheese from abroad, and very little fruit of any kind that the English climate could produce. In estimating the loss of foreign trade, as Mr. Oliphant pointed out, people forget the loss and the waste, which comes from foreigners rushing in with their supplies of what England could very well produce. The labor on the main crops, the cereals, was economised very much by steam ploughs and reapers, but the more minute labor in the minor industries, the weeding and hoeing and gathering, was very great.

"Are women as well as men employed in agricultural work," I asked.

"Certainly," said Mr. Oliphant, "there would not otherwise be enough for the female contingent to do on the Ossulton farm, and our women must work as well as our men."

"Are all the laborers housed in this single home for the work of this large farm."

"No; there are two homes, each containing about 120 souls, located at convenient distance, so that no worker is very far from his work."

"That is a great deal of labor for the land according to Australian practice, but not as much as was bestowed on it before the days of machinery in England. I do not see how you can employ more people in agriculture than they used to do a hundred years ago."

"We do indeed, because the whole country is cultivated in the same minute way. There is not half of the pasture land to the arable that there used to be, and wastes and moors and marshes have been reclaimed, parks and pleasure grounds in private occupation taken into cultivation, though indeed parks and recreation grounds for the people have been enlarged and multiplied everywhere; but that does not amount to half the other."

CHAPTER III 63

"Our Australian cultivation was of course wheat, wheat, wheat, which was to be called the pioneer crop, grown with the least cost of labor of any crop, especially in a new country. And it was held that it was far cheaper for England to import food to supply her manufacturing population, and to pay for this by export of manufactured goods than to grow it on her own limited soil."

"But when the outside world would have none of her exports, what then? We had to do the best we could with our own soil."

"And seeing the crops you grow, the best is certainly pretty satisfactory."

"Why the dependence on foreign food paralysed all legitimate efforts at the development of agriculture. Land in the hands of terrified and indebted proprietors, who saw their rents decrease and the burdens on the land in no way decrease, could never be done justice to. English capital would go to the ends of the world buying gold mines or silver claims or lending to insolvent States--anywhere rather than on the soil of England. Emigration took the pick of our young men and left us with the feeble and the feckless, with women who competed with men and each other at the worst-paid and least-healthy of employments, with lunatics and criminals and paupers draining the life-blood out of the country. The England you knew did not become the mother of nations without many bitter pangs that threatened to be death-throes."

"What a Protectionist you are! I was brought up a Free Trader," I said, amazed at Mr. Oliphant's deprecation of what had been the pride and boast of my own day.

"It was a great step in evolution. Much was taught by Adam Smith and his followers even more valuable than Free Trade. They helped us to get at the roots of things."

I was puzzled, but I could not but confess that whatever might have been the cause, the result in quantity of crop as well as in the general well-being of the laborers was very satisfactory. The careless cultivation of Australia with which I was most familiar, of course was nowhere as compared to this, but even the best which I had seen in

CHAPTER III

England and East Lothian halted far behind, especially in the variety of produce. Was this indeed the English agricultural laborer, with his slow bovine glance exchanged for a look of keen intelligence, who directed the reaping machine or disposed of the sheaves? Was this old man of seventy still able to tend cattle and feed the horses, his joints now unracked by rheumatism, hale and upright, with the winter apple complexion on his cheeks, and either his own teeth or those supplied by art, fair and even in his head? When I sat down by the side of Mr. George Oliphant at the mid-day meal with one half of his laborers I felt the social revolution more strongly than ever. They were in their working clothes, with thick boots, and a trifle dusty from the harvest-field, but a finer lot of men and women I never saw, and their manners, though not quite as good as those of the Owen Home, were courteous yet independent. I sat beside on the other hand the oldest inhabitant, who would have been a toothless, bed-ridden, old crone, but who now with a snow-white cap on her head, and a complete set of teeth inside of it, talked to me as a stranger from Australia rather condescendingly, on account of her great age, putting me just a little in mind of my own mother.

These laborers had no longer cold, damp hovels to live in, and insufficient food, and clothing not fitted to protect them from the changes of weather. The food was as good as at the Owen Home. Not only was there a substantial advance in diet from the agricultural laborer of England, but the American farmer and Australian selector had not as good or as varied a diet, and nothing like the comfort in eating it which these co-operative agriculturalists enjoyed. The service was all done by members of the home and exclusively by women. This was an outlet for a large contingent, and the dairy and poultry-yard took others. In winter, when there was little or no field work, though by organisation almost all the men and boys were constantly employed, the women took to their by-trades. One woman with a knitting machine knitted the stockings and socks for the community, and another the guernseys worn by the men. All the underclothes, all the tailoring, and all the dressmaking of the little community for the year were made in the winter, and all the house repairs and supplies of furniture needed. Baskets were made of osiers grown on the farm, and all the twine and rope needed for the establishment were made in the winter months. The flax and hemp occupied some, but the beet was sold in bulk to the sugar factories.

The home-brewed beer was excellent, light, and deliciously fresh, made of malt and hops grown on the farm. There was also cider for those who preferred it. I found fewer teetotallers at the Ossulton Home than at the Owen Home, but that was perhaps because it was harvest time. The cookery was not quite so delicate, but it was exceedingly good.

What a contrast from the laborer of the past, subsisting on day's wages, with no look-out for old age but the work-house, touching his hat humbly to every well-dressed person he met and eager to open a gate or a carriage-door in hopes of a stray penny or sixpence from the gentlefolks.

Every man and woman here had a share--a small one certainly--in the farm. They felt it to be their own. They handled the costly machines with an owner's pride and intelligent care. They watched that there should be no waste to take from their gains. The fruit trees were their own--no boy robbed them; the animals were their own--it was everybody's interest to be kind to them; every tool and implement they used was their own--it must be taken care of and repaired on the first sign of needing it.

"I see a great deal of vegetable and fruit farming besides what you need for your own consumption," said I to Mr. George Oliphant. If all the homes are as well supplied as the Owen Home I cannot see where your market can be."

"Homes in towns and cities cannot obtain so much ground as in the suburbs. We send our produce by railway to London."

The manager of the farm could scarcely understand my desire for statistics of the produce and the cost of cultivation of Ossulton. I could gather that of the old crops the produce per acre was about 20 per cent. larger than in the individual capitalist farming days, and that the value of the minor products, which had been virtually neglected, was about one-eighth of the whole, so there was an addition of 30 to 40 per cent. to the produce, and on Ossulton an addition of 300 acres which

CHAPTER III 66

was waste land before. As for cost of cultivation, the cost for machinery was much greater, and that for labor somewhat more than before, but as each of the hands had capital in the concern he drew out first his wages, next interest calculated at 2½ per cent. on the capital, and lastly his share in the profits.

The capital in the first place had been found by the workers foregoing part of the ordinary wages, partly by the profits on co-operative consumption.

I asked if the two Ossulton homes were proprietary like the Owen, and was told that they were partly so. Some owned their standing in it, and some paid rent, but of the latter the purchase money was gradually extinguished by paying more rent than sufficed to pay interest on the outlay and repairs.

The Home was not so beautiful as the Owen, and not so full of decorations and old fashioned relics of the past, but it was roomy and comfortable. It was on the whole more cheaply conducted, and the land on which it stood was of course only taken at its value for agriculture, whereas the Hampstead land was costly. But even that was bought, and the Associated Home built and furnished with help such as I have mentioned, at a cost of £10,000, which made £500 the price of a permanent family home. This with interest so low as it was in England at the time I visited it, made a very cheap home even to rent, particularly considering what it included. The Ossulton Homes cost about £400 for each family, and as the families averaged three or four adult workers, the rent was no heavy strain on their earnings.

I had seen whole streets in London, in which the rent of a single room was 5s. a-week, and in which many working families could not afford more.

How many times did I wish that I could have had more than a week in the future. I had to leave my agricultural home when dinner ended, and take the train for a manufacturing town a little further from London where Mr. Edward Carmichael lived. I found the cotton factory in the middle of the second shift. Were these the modern representatives of the girls I had seen in 1866, with unkempt hair and a shawl over their

CHAPTER III

heads, and soiled and untidy gowns, who, with loud laugh or vacant smile, hurried to and from their long day's work at the mill,--these bright intelligent girls, or rather married women, for most of them wore wedding rings, who stood over their looms or watched the bobbins with so much interest in their work? And had they really an interest--a pecuniary interest I mean--in the thread as it was spun, and the web as it was woven? All the hands in the mill, the manager told me (with some surprise at the question even from a benighted person from the Antipodes) had this interest in the profits, larger or smaller as the amount of capital was large or small which invested, but absolutely irrefragable in respect of the work done. The capital was sometimes put in by the parents, but more generally accumulated by the younger members by taking what we were used to call 'subsist' wages for several years.

"But what if you make losses instead of profits, the hands must take their share of them too?"

"Certainly, if we make losses, they must, but we have never made any yet."

"The market is so certain," said my friend Mr. Oliphant, "And the prices fixed rather by custom than by competition. This mill is exclusively for home consumption. The export trade, which is still large, is carried on chiefly from Manchester and the Lancashire mills. I do not know that Edward can answer all your questions, but I think I am correct when I say that this mill worked by three thousand operatives in three shifts daily, has an output equal to that of an old mill with two thousand five hundred operatives for an ordinary day. The machinery costs a good deal less than it did; the interest on capital is lower; the market is steady, and----"

"People pay more for the calico and muslin," I interrupted.

"I do not think the consumer pays any more. Recollect that all the profits and the risks of the middlemen are saved. I believe the commodity is quite as cheap one year with another, and you see the condition of the workpeople."

CHAPTER III

"It is as good as Mr. Daniel Pidgeon's account of the New England factory hands--better than the Lowell girls had; they had far longer hours, and I am sure, plainer fare."

"Plain living and high thinking were classed together sometimes." said Mr. Oliphant.

"But I see a very large proportion of women and girls here," I said. "Is this what some New England writer called a she-town, where the men had to live on the labor of their wives, and sisters, and daughters, or to emigrate elsewhere?"

"The men are employed partly in the iron and metal works of this town."

"You have no young children in the mill?"

"No, we never take any hands under fourteen, when their elementary education is finished."

"And what do your people do with the rest of their time if they only work six hours for you?" I asked Mr. Carmichael. That question was always on my lips.

"Well, I suppose they use it for living," said he, with a slight elevation of his eyebrows.

I recollected the answer made by a large cotton manufacturer, early in my own century, when a foreign visitor asked him "If these wretched dwellings, in Manchester, was where his workpeople lived?" "No," said he, "they only sleep there, they live in my mill." I did not quote it aloud, lest I should make Mr. Carmichael still more surprised. He went on to say:

"They use their leisure, as we all do, for their own personal pleasure, and for the general beautifying of life. Every one who has a hobby cultivates it. We have had mechanical inventions and appliances from one, economy in lighting from another, hints on ventilation from a third. That fair-haired girl you see at your left, draws and paints very well, the dark-eyed one you noticed first, writes poetry. The entertainments they get up in their homes take a good deal of study and preparation; and, of course, they are all musical, whatever they are not. Oh! there is no difficulty in getting rid of eighteen hours a day, with meals, sleep, recreation, and self-improvement--an intelligent pursuit of happiness is the object of life; you cannot dispute that in Adelaide, or elsewhere."

"I do not think I ever heard it stated so boldly. Happiness should come indirectly. I have always been exhorted to a diligent pursuit of virtue. Happiness may, or may not, accompany it, but the virtue was indispensable."

"But virtue requires you to seek and to labor for the happiness of others." said Edward Carmichael. "Is it not better for them to seek it for themselves, they know better what they want. Happiness depends more on ourselves than on any one else certainly. The intelligent pursuit of happiness on the part of each individual is, of course, limited by the intelligent pursuit of happiness by all those around him, with whom he comes in contact, both for business and pleasure."

"Then this direct pursuit of happiness does not lead to selfishness?"

"I don't think so; for if we encroach on the rights, or hurt the feelings of other people, they soon let us know, and all outsiders will back them up. This is what makes it possible to keep order among so many workers as I can do. Every one knows the rules, and every one is interested in seeing that they are obeyed."

"Now," said Mr. Oliphant, as we departed, "you should see a large co-operative distribution store."

"I have seen such things, and read about them a great deal. The Civil Service and the Army and Navy stores were quite great establishments."

"Oh! these were cheap-selling stores, not saving stores, like those established by the Rochdale pioneers, and copied all over the North of England. Even these were not true to their original traditions. I shall take you to one which the Owen Home deals at--proprietary stores,

CHAPTER III

where all those who buy and all those who sell have a vested interest."

I was taken to this great Emporium, and noted how little was expended for show either in the building or the get-up of the goods. All goods were bought first-hand at the lowest remunerative prices. There were no show-cases, no useless decorations, no fancy boxes with colored pictures, of more or less merit, to make the contents attractive. I priced several articles, and while I noted that many necessary and useful things were cheaper, a great many of the minor conveniences and little luxuries of life were dearer. I did not regret to see that lucifer matches--for which there was now a limited demand--were much more expensive than they were, so that they would not be so wastefully and recklessly used. It was the endeavor of the London manufacturers to compete with the cheap production of Sweden that brought down the price, while the miserable match-box makers lived in rags and dirt in London slums and the unhealthy fumes shortened the lives of the matchmakers themselves.

There must have been great displacement of industry everywhere. The girls who earned a living by making fancy boxes, and by drawing and designing pictures for them, had no successors now-a-days. Christmas and birthday cards, too, had gone out. I understood that everything was to be had at the stores, from a needle to an anchor, from a dancing shoe to a ton of coals, but when I asked for birthday cards, the shopman stared at me.

I was tired and hungry, but happy, when I reached the Owen Home, with Mr. Oliphant, in time for the evening meal.

I spent an hour in the music room, and found that Wagner's was not really the music of the future, for no one seemed to have heard of him. Handel, Mozart, Beethoven, and Mendelsohn (sic) were still known and loved. I felt at first as if the music of the *post nati* was far from me and my sympathies, but gradually it won upon me. A subtle sense, now of excitement, now of sorrow, now of repose, now of joy, crept over me. The part-singing was perfect, for the voices had practised together all their lives. There were at least four quite new musical instruments, but the pride of the Home was one matchless old Straduarius (sic), thrown into the common property, in 1900, by a musical member. Yes, whatever might be the case with other arts, music had certainly advanced.

After an hour's music I quitted the room rather reluctantly to go with Mrs. Carmichael into the art room where I saw people of all ages, and of both sexes, but mostly younger members, drawing from models and modelling in clay, while reading aloud went on.

The book read related to their studies and pursuits, for it was a History of Art, but the period had got beyond my day, and it was difficult for me to follow it, but I saw great fidelity and rapidity of execution in the hands that practised art in the Owen Home. I heard of sketching parties planned for Saturday afternoon, which--even with the short hours of labor--appeared to be somewhat of a half-holiday.

I next went into the card-room, and played with a Mr. Barton,--who had travelled in the interior of Africa, and who was very interesting, (but I cannot write half of what I saw,)--with Mrs. Oliphant and a great friend of hers, a Mr. Robert Somerville, at a modification of whist, in which I needed some instruction, but showed myself fairly apt.

I then went to my own room and wrote down what I could recollect of this day, which appeared only less wonderful than the preceding one. I was getting used to my century--that was all.

CHAPTER IV

WEDNESDAY

Childhood and Education

My programme for Wednesday was to observe and study the development and training of children in the nursery, in the home, in the school, in the playground, and in such apprenticeship to industrial life as was required in the society of the future. In this Mrs. Oliphant was my guide for the earlier part of the day.

When associated homes were first started, the idea that each home should contain school-rooms and have teachers was held in great favor, but the difficulty of grading the limited number of all ages made this too costly for anything but elementary or early education. The State provided free schools with trained teachers, but did not take children under eight years old. I objected to this that it must be impossible for all people everywhere to live in associated homes. In remote districts there must be solitary shepherds, herdsmen and fishermen, able to earn a livelihood, but unable to combine with others. I was told that in cases where I should have thought it quite impossible, two, three or four families joined in housekeeping and divided the duties amongst them. Economy and comfort led to this organisation. Even where there were solitary families, the parents had all received sufficient education to teach their children what was necessary to fit them for the public schools.

In the school-rooms belonging to each home the children of the associated families received instruction in reading, writing and simple calculation, and above all in knowledge of things as distinguished from knowledge of words. The nursery teaching was thoroughly natural and delightful in the manner in which each lesson in knowledge and in skill was felt to be learned as much by the learner's own intellectual or artistic effort as by the teacher's guidance. I could see how early the lesson of bearing and forbearing, of respect for the rights of others, was inculcated without needing any severe punishment or risking any nervous shock to the delicate organisation of a young infant or little child.

CHAPTER IV

In the nursery stood a baby prison-house. It was a good sized circular basket, weighted so that it could not be overturned, and softly lined and cushioned. A baby creeps to some forbidden place, inconvenient to others and dangerous to himself. He is gently removed. He creeps there again and again. The nurse lifts him quietly and gently, places him in the basket and gives him toys. There he remains till the impulse to disobey has worn itself out; the attraction has been forgotten. The child of two, flings his ball in baby's face, and though conscious of the wrong-doing, persists in the amusement. He is firmly placed in the basket, where he lies down to kick or scream till he is tired or contrite. When these children pass out of the nursery their nerves are healthy and strong. They know no craven fear, for gentle kindness has formed the moral atmosphere they have breathed. They are trained to docility and prompt obedience, and understand perfectly the simple principle that if they abuse liberty, their liberty will be abridged. They are sensitive in a high degree to affection, for love has surrounded them, and from the very dawn of consciousness formed the one stimulus to painful effort, and to successful effort the natural and abundant reward.

"From our very birth, you see," said Mrs. Oliphant, "we are hemmed in by authority which, though it does not repress spontaneous action, checks all encroachments on the rights of others. There are very few forbidden things in this nursery, nothing too fine to be touched, and very early children are given things to play with that they exercise their activity in."

"Like what we had in the Kindergarten system," said I.

"Yes, modified and amplified. The very first lesson in morals they learn is kindness to animals. It is surprising how much a sympathetic mother or nurse can inspire, but some masterful children have their longest experience of our basket prison and similar punishments to check their disposition to play too roughly or cruelly with the kitten, or to take off the wings of flies."

"With so many children grouped together in a common nursery, I should fear that personal rights of property would be rather hard to understand and enforce."

CHAPTER IV 74

"We do not live in such a community as this. As we have our own apartments, and our own clothes and furniture, so the children in this common nursery have their own property, even though some out-grown toys descend. Some things are no doubt for common use, and children have their turn, but most of the toys, such as dolls and balls, and bats and tops, are private property which the other children may borrow with consent of the owner, but must not touch without it. Of course you see how important it is that this lesson should be taught early. All the advantages of Associated Homes, and of the Co-operative system generally, can only be enjoyed by keeping up constant respect for each other's rights and feelings. And this lesson is continuously taught, not only in the nursery and the home, but in the school, on the playground, and in the workshop and factory"

"My experience was that there was one discipline for the school, another for the home, and another for the playground, but all too much on the basis that nothing succeeds like success, the race to the swift, and the battle to the strong. The church was weak as against this teaching. Can you possibly equalise human conditions when human beings are so unequal?"

"We can smooth away all artificial causes of disparity. We can make the race one in which all can win something, and that which is won, not taken from the losers. We can give a new reading to that hard old text, that from him who hath not, shall be taken away that which he hath. That is, we deprive of liberty our moral failures. The power of doing mischief, where the nature is so depraved as to be irreclaimable, must be taken away."

I watched the two nurses in charge of about thirty children under fourteen; half of them went to the State school. This looks a small proportion of children for twenty families, and for some children of attendants besides, some of whom included, like Mrs. Carmichael's three generations, but in her case there were no young children at all, and this was the case with several others; and no family is allowed to exceed three children. One of the nurses was the teacher of the younger children. There were only two babies in the Owen Home, and the elder children seemed to be very fond of them.

CHAPTER IV

I have seen Kindergarten teaching, but this was more varied and on the whole more useful. The use of the hands was taught before the little ones learned to read, but the education of the eye and of the ear, was earlier still. In the walks which the children took in the garden, and in the nearest park, they were taught to look out for beautiful things, to watch the plants grow, and the flowers expand, to note the changes in the sky, and the ripples in the lake, to be observant of the ways of the dumb animals, to learn what these liked, and if possible to please them, to help each other, and to trust each other. Fear, the mother of falsehood, was absent from their training, but the playful sallies of a child's imagination were not repressed. The perfect justice and fairness, with which the children were treated, gave little occasion for jealousy and envy; the education of the feelings was carried on constantly, directly, but far more indirectly.

I saw now clearly, how much the militant spirit had penetrated society. Even in my own day, when we professed to be a peace-loving Christian nation, and also an industrial community, it had lived in trade in its fierce competition--it had lived in sport, in the slaying of innocent creatures for pleasure, and in the gambling and betting upon every kind of contest of strength and skill in men or animals; it had lived in school life through the prize system and competitive examinations, and had been feebly repressed by the best home influences, and the highest religious ideals.

In this society made up of equals, two children belonging to Mr. and Mrs. Cox, who were the resident attendants bound to sleep on the place, were, with the children of the members of the home, on exactly the same footing, as well as four young children belonging to other employés, who were at the Owen Home during the day, but went to other homes with their parents at night. The whole force of public opinion, which is really the collective conscience, and has varied according to the degree of civilization the community has arrived at, was brought to bear on children and young people with an even and uniform pressure. It was held that not to be a productive laborer in one form or another was a disgrace, instead of, as in my own childhood, that respectability, gentility, or whatever other word might be used to distinguish the status of the better classes, demanded our being absolved from all manual labor. Sensible as my mother was, sensible

CHAPTER IV

as I thought myself, the society of the leisured and educated classes was so much pleasanter than that of the toilers who produced the wealth and comfort that others lived in, that, insensibly, we looked down on the latter, or rather we expected them to look up to us. There was much kindly feeling towards them, and a great desire to better their condition, but not that *respect humain* that permeated all society a hundred years after my day. Their betters were to teach them, to help them, and in various ways to patronise the lower orders, and, no doubt, that was an important transition stage from the earlier and harsher--to "exploit" them as the feudal born did his serfs, the planter his slaves, the mill-owner his hands, for his own convenience and profit only. But the patronage was unluckily often full of suspicion on one side, and tempted to falsehood, exaggeration, and dissimulation, if not hypocrisy, on the other. How often have I in despair thought that charity was the most difficult of the virtues to practice, and the most dangerous of virtues to society. That it needed more of the wisdom of the serpent than of the harmlessness of the dove, for unwise charity often proves the most insidious kind of cruelty. What we held as the playful sketch by Praed of the kindly cynic Quince,

Who held a maxim, that the poor Were always able, never willing; And so the beggar at his door Had first abuse, and then a shilling. Asylums, hospitals, and schools, He swore, were only meant to cozen; All who subscribed to them were fools, And he subscribed to half a dozen

was foreign to all the feelings and principles of the twentieth century. The poor man, i.e. the working man, would be as much insulted by the shilling as by the abuse, and would condone no abuse for any amount of money. The asylums, hospitals and schools, which existed still, were supported by the community with even and not fitful "liberality", instead of being a heavy burden on the benevolent portion of the public. A Scrooge, if any such existed, could not now excuse himself from payment of the general burden by saying that he paid compulsorily to maintain the work-house, for that institution no longer existed.

From the nursery lessons I went on to the State school, at which children attended from the age of eight till the age of 14. Here all classes are mingled even more than in the homes, where affinities

CHAPTER IV   77

generally made people of hereditary culture join in housekeeping, especially at the date when most of the associated homes were founded. In 1900 there were much greater differences between the professional classes and the manual workers than in 1987. In the schools, the most perfect equality prevailed; boys and girls were taught together, which I had always approved of, as it makes them quicker and brighter and more courteous. The literary education seemed to me to be less extensive than in our better schools, but the education in science was much more thorough, and both boys and girls learned the use of their hands; so that a young person of 14 was not as raw a hand for industrial life as the child of 13 out of board schools, nor had he or she the same objection to manual labor which our present bright scholars show. The great proportion went at once to work, but in the abundant leisure there was plenty of opportunity for continuing education, and there was help offered on every hand in the pursuit of knowledge. A taste for reading was very general, but it was not universal. I could not, however, fancy lads and girls leaving the teaching of the nursery and of the National school without a taste for something more than amusement.

School hours were not over long, and school duties were not made irksome and anxious by the constant effort to turn out show pupils on the one side, and on the other to impart the required minimum of instruction to reluctant and recalcitrant children. School holidays were few and short compared to those of our time, when the hard-working teachers and pupils needed long holidays. The lazy and indifferent abuse them, and especially in the case of boarding schools the idleness and license of long holidays often made parents dread them. Boarding schools were now altogether exploded, and the continuity of instruction and discipline was not rudely broken several times in the year. There was little harshnesss in school management, and children were expected to occupy themselves, and not make themselves an infliction during the short holiday time, in the twentieth century. When pupils did wrong, the teachers assumed that it arose from ignorance of what was right or from weakness of self-control, and every encouragement was given that might strengthen the conscience and rightly direct the will. The idea of breaking a child's will, such as good Susannah Wesley and thousands of other parents thought the first duty towards it, was absolutely repugnant to parents, nurses, teachers,

CHAPTER IV 78

and preachers now-a-days. The will is the character, the very ego of each individual; it can be influenced by love and by reason, but it must be held sacred from violence and arbitrary power. In the school playground, I noticed that the pupils themselves elected their monitors and prefects, who kept order. The teacher was the last resort, but was seldom called in. As the National school had no infant teaching or elementary teaching, the requirements were high and not wasted. I did not see the Continuation schools for myself, but these were so largely carried on during leisure hours by voluntary efforts on the part of teachers and taught, that they did not cost the State much. There were a few advanced schools where parents paid for special training. Through one of these Florrie Oliphant had passed, and she was now going on with her studies at the University where she had met with her fate in the person of Fred Steele.

She was qualifying herself for teaching in the National schools--perhaps she was ambitious of rising to higher walks, but that would be attained by private study. Her lover was to be an engineer, and had to go through a good deal of hard practical work as well as the University training. I went to the London University, which was no longer an examining body merely, but a teaching body as well, and saw the mixed classes of youths and maidens, or what would have been maidens in our time. But I learned that Florrie's case was not exceptional, but that many marriages took place in student life--perhaps, on the whole, a better arena for matrimonial choice than the ball room.

At the university I observed that though the masters and mistressses, the professors and lecturers, male and female, were supreme in all that regarded instruction, they resigned authority to the young people themselves, not singly, but in their corporate or collective capacity to regulate conduct and to discipline the turbulent elements within their circle. The students elected conducted committees from their number, and these committees were generally warmly supported. If at any time they were felt to be faulty, over-harsh or over-lax, next year's election made a change in the *personnel*, which, besides, changed as the students left the university and entered the world. Youthful public opinion in both school and university was enlisted and exercised for the protection of the weak and the maintenance of good order. The

CHAPTER IV

youthful generation thus learned practically the science of sociology before they took their active part as adults in the business of the world.

The prizes at school, like the prizes of life, used to be won from defeated and mortified competitors. Over and over again I have seen boys, and girls too (though not quite so markedly in their case) work for prizes at school, carry them off, and then forget all the knowledge which such prizes had been held to be the only means of making them acquire. In the schools and universities which were now under my eye, the love of knowledge, the desire for skill, the delight in observation, furnished a motive power which surprised me. The prayer of the intellect--which is attention--was answered by the highest of intellectual pleasures--the conquest of a difficulty. Every new acquisition of knowledge was welded into previous knowledge and linked with it so that it never could be forgotten. Combined with this was the real liking that subsisted between teachers and pupils, leading to the mental effort which the system of punishments and prizes only succeeded in stimulating in a few who might have made it without. Sir Walter Scott says:--

You call this education, do you not? Why, 'tis the forced march of a herd of bullocks Before a shouting drover. The glad van Move on at ease, and pause a while to snatch A passing morsel from the scanty sward! While all the oaths, blows, imprecations, Fall on the head of the unlucky laggards That cripple in the rear.

I saw that children were much dearer to their parents when there were fewer of them. They were not felt as the burden and anxiety that they were in the last quarter of the nineteenth century. Parents, not overworked or over anxious, could give and did give a great part of their leisure to their children, but neither father nor mother lived altogether in the nursery. Mrs. Oliphant said that while her children were young she undertook less professional work, and shut off her outside interests in a great measure, and that the happiest hours of her life had been spent with the little ones and her husband in a family life as perfect as could be enjoyed at any time. The grandfather and grandmother often joined them and had perfect liberty to have the children's society for certain hours of the day in their own apartments, but only when they wished it.

CHAPTER IV											80

"I think," said she, "that the walks we had with the little ones were as helpful to them as any of their school lessons. You know what a gardener and florist Mr. Oliphant is. My turn is for animated nature, so the children learned from us much about plants and animals."

"Parents now-a-days seem never to ask the anxious question: What shall we do with our boys? What shall we do with our girls?" I said.

"Why should we?" said Mrs. Oliphant calmly. "The boys will fill their fathers' places, the girls lead the same life as their mothers--that is, with reasonable allowance for difference of temperament and abilities. Florrie prefers teaching to medicine--considers medicine is a profession that is on the decline, so I do not object. My son, who is travelling, is picking up information and ideas which will make him useful on the staff of the *Daily News*--and it is his wish to be a journalist. His elder brother had not any taste for that line of life."

"Of course," said I, "the smallness of your families is the cause of your ease in the present and your ease for the future. When a man saw four sons growing up to compete with him in industrial pursuits, lowering the wages beyond what would maintain a family, so that even married women had to leave young children to eke out the family income, things were very different. I have heard a woman, not unmotherly, but schooled by such hard facts, say, 'I have a long family, but, thank God, the church-yard has stood my friend. I had only six that lived to be doing for themselves.'"

"We like to keep all our children alive," said Mrs. Oliphant.

"Your young people are, I hope as eager in their play as in their studies," I said.

"I think they are. It is curious that the only thing that competition enters much into is athletic sports. It is still a pride and triumph to run faster and farther, to jump higher, to wheel faster than our compeers, and to win games and matches in bodies and clubs."

"I see your young people are very well and evenly developed. The race, generally, seems taller and heavier since I saw the world."

CHAPTER IV

"Yes, it is. Statistics prove this, not only from the dying-out of the old, ill-fed, hereditary poor, but even those who correspond to the middle and upper classes, who, if you recollect, were so much larger than their ancestors that mediaeval armour could not be worn by the average Briton at the Eglinton tournament, are still larger and finer."

"But you have no field sports such as developed these classes in my day."

"Not connected with killing, certainly," said Mrs. Oliphant.

"The Briton, young or middle-aged, in want of a sensation used to say: 'Come, let us kill something,' and certainly, his own health was the better for the enforced fatigue and hardship of many field sports, hunting, coursing, deer-stalking and the like."

"Sports which are pursued on horseback are out of date now, as too costly for our social condition, but every home by the sea or near the river can maintain a boat--and boating is a most popular exercise. Cycling is quite within our means and is universal. The old games of cricket and football and tennis still exist with some modifications, and a dozen new games of skill and speed have been invented for boys and girls, sometimes separated, sometimes mixed.

"Saturday afternoon is the great recreation time. We have the cheapest trains running, and towns folk go to the country and country folk to towns to try each other's mettle." "Have you any horse races now? Is the Derby day a thing of the past?"

"It is."

"The racecourses of England, of course, were the outcome of a wealthy and luxurious people, and a great competition between them was a spectacle even for poorer folks." "Say of a gambling people," said Mrs. Oliphant.

"Without the bets the interest in the noble animal would have been limited to a few."

CHAPTER IV

"But in America the popular races were trotting matches, which Dr. Holmes used to call the 'sport for a democratic people'--a good trotter was useful, a racehorse was simply ornamental."

"We are too democratic for even trotting matches."

"But people in my day betted on everything. The horse race was, certainly the most organised of betting rings, with the bookmakers always *contra*, and the gudgeon public always *pro*, but every contest lent itself to gambling."

"Where the gambling spirit is, it finds outlets everywhere, no doubt," said Mrs. Oliphant.

"Is it dead now? That is impossible!"

"Well, it seems as if it was perishing of inanition. When society was reconstructed, bookmakers and other vermin who preyed on the weakness and the credulity of society were dealt with as rogues and vagabonds. Many of them were driven into industrial life, many, indeed, had talents which, rightly directed, were useful."

"The difficulty of getting a living by regular work, and the easiness of getting a better living without it, tempted not only the vicious into evil ways," said I.

"When you extirpate the professional gambler you do a great deal to discourage the amateur. The security and permanence of our social system work steadily against the gambling spirit."

"But, the Stock Exchange--the Corners--the Time Bargains!--all these were arenas for gambling in a large way."

"You would not know the Stock Exchange again. Mr. Oliphant would tell you better than I can how the direct method of buying and selling cuts off not only the profits of the middlemen, but those of the speculator."

CHAPTER IV

"No doubt your system of training and education succeeds splendidly with the average, but what about your failures? While human nature is so mixed and complex, there must be failures. You make short work with one class, the congenital idiots, but these are few."

"Very few. Healthy parents rarely have idiot children, and teething rarely causes brain diseases of permanent type."

"Then the old pauper class?"

"Has died out with the system which gave it birth. The adults were incorrigible, but we struck at the roots and determined that no child should be brought up a pauper."

"That work was begun in my day," said I. "I took an active part in it in my corner of the world, and was surprised at the success of training against heredity. But heredity left some failures with us, and must have left more in such a country as England."

"They drifted into vice and crime here and there, but while we were training the young we stopped the demoralising relief for the older. The progress of Society made it more and more difficult for a criminal career to be carried on--detection became more and more scientific and more certain. The stupid criminal was easily caught and reformed, if possible, by being taught an honest calling.

"The clever baffled us longer, but the pauper *sui generis*, who would contentedly live in idleness on the earnings of other people was what society could not and would not tolerate. He was made to work for the *whole* of his maintenance, if he sought shelter in the work-house, and he preferred to do this at liberty."

"Then your criminals--?"

"When our children of all classes had received the careful training and education which we consider best fitted to draw out the higher, and to repress the lower nature, then, and not till then, do criminals stand out convicted of moral insanity, and thus, too, not a first or a second lapse into crime. A large proportion are saved to society by the probation system, but the residue are dealt with like other dangerous lunatics, fed, clothed and employed, even amused, but not allowed to prey on society or to perpetuate the species. In direct contrast to mediaeval celibacy, which prevented the parenthood of some of the sweetest and wisest of the race, the mischievous and morally diseased are debarred from it."

"You will then have a decreasing rate of crime."

"Yes, and of lunacy as well. So many of the predisposing causes of crimes are removed in the rewards of honest industry being so certain. Lunacy is not fed by intemperance, prostitution and gambling, or by the fierce alternations of fortune. A man does not work at his desk till he drops in order to add thousands to his already large capital, or to keep thousands from being lost for want of the present vigilance which was required. The struggling tradesman used to have as hard a fight to hold up his head against fierce competition; the artisan or laborer was liable to weeks or months of the year of no employment, the community losing what he might have produced, and he, meanwhile, living or half starving on his savings, which ought to have been kept for the time when he was past work, or on charity. Life is now so much pleasanter and more secure that lunacy is rare, and suicide is almost unheard of, except in cases of lunacy, when it is never interfered with after hope of recovery is over."

"Many of the best institutions of my time seem to be extinguished as well as the worst. Where are the orphan asylums?" said I.

"We do not need orphan asylums where families are so small and the average life so long. When there chance to be real orphans, uncles and aunts generally adopt them, or they are eagerly sought for by childless parents. Sometimes they are laid hold of by the home in which they were born, and belong to the twenty families collectively, who, if no sufficient means have been left by parents, contribute for their maintenance."

"Then the countless asylums for old people in almshouses and hospitals?"

CHAPTER IV

"These are still less needed. It is the universal custom which has all the force of law without its harshness to make savings for old age, though not for children as able and as willing to work as their parents. The reciprocal duties of children to parents are expressed by public opinion as strongly as the primary duty of parents to children, so that the failing health of old people receives personal attention, though their own friends provide for their support."

"Are there no hospitals now?"

"Certainly, for some acute and severe illnesses and for accidents; we have hospitals in towns and cities, but as you may see the Associated Home has in it sufficient appliances for tending most of the sicknesses to which humanity is now subject. I rarely have to send a case to the hospital, but I consider my hospital practice of use to me."

"The list of diseases used to change in my time. Some old scourges were stamped out, or in process of being so, but new maladies, chiefly, I think, nervous, became more and more prevalent. In my day we heard first of cholera in Europe, and diphtheria (if not the same as the old putrid sore throat), was a new disease and a fatal one."

"On its preventive side I think medicine has made most progress of all," said Mrs. Oliphant. "Cholera and small-pox are extirpated as well as scarletina (sic), measles and whooping-cough. And hygiene and sanitation have put an end to typhoid and allied fevers."

"I am not surprised to hear you say that your profession is declining. It has been too clever for its own interests."

"Instead of sickness being a costly and often unprepared-for contingency, it is now reduced to a matter of sheer calculation and included in the expenses of the associated home. The contribution for each family is so small that it is felt no burden, while it takes off the pressure on the suffering individual."

"This is an extension of the old Friendly Society or Lodge in which all prudent artisans insured against sickness. Only if he was out of work, and as they called it, *bad in the books*--in arrears with his weekly shilling or sixpence, he lost all benefit from his past payments. Of course a sick person loses his wages for his maintenance, and may fall into arrears in his payment for board and maintenance in his home."

"The same spirit of collectiveness and mutual assurance runs through all our social system. Very rarely does sickness come when there are not sufficient savings to meet it, and if not the arrears are made up afterwards. It is, of course, my interest as well as my pleasure to keep down the rate of sickness in the houses I contract to attend. My modest income is not swelled by protracted illness, nor by ministering to the fancy of rich *malades imaginaires*."

Returning to the matter of education, I found the nation paid all the cost of primary education out of national revenues. It also supported the universities, but I was surprised to find that the continuation schools, the link between the public schools and the university, were attended mostly by people engaged in bread-winning occupations, and taught by others similarly engaged. An intelligent community furnished enough of recruits eager to learn and eager to teach. Science had made great strides both in the hold it had taken on the general intelligence and in the discoveries and applications of specialists.

I asked Mrs. Oliphant if education, given by the State, was free, compulsory and secular.

"It was free, no fees were demanded of any one, it was compulsory without the aid of law because public opinion expressed it. As to its being secular, the education of the conscience and the feelings was so continuously carried on that nothing seemed secular which concerned the duties and the happiness of ourselves and our fellows. The lessons of the school coincided with those of the home and of the church, but religious or scriptural education was carried on by other agencies."

I asked my informant, "How do you inspect and prove the teaching which is thus paid for by the nation? Is there not a risk of the uniform-teaching system becoming, if it has not already become, a dull mechanical drill?"

CHAPTER IV
87

"The national inspectors who are needed to keep well-paid employés up to their duties require results but do not prescribe methods, so that the modes of imparting knowledge and drawing out intelligence are various, and this makes school-work more interesting. If you had seen the early teaching at the Ossulton Home you would have found it different in many points from that of the Owen Home, but the children leave these with the beginning of your old three R's taught them, able to sing and to dance, accustomed to drill, to obedience, order and good manners."

"I am much struck with the good manners everywhere," said I, "especially those of the young to the old. I feel a little ashamed of myself because I objected last week to joint housekeeping for the sake of economy, because, though I might like the lady herself, her nephews and nieces were objectionable to me, and some of her friends were, what is called, bores. How do so many families live together without friction, and so many generations of the same family, which is, perhaps, more difficult still?"

"We had to make rules as to intrusion on privacy of strangers, and these were found to be equally important for blood relations, and for relatives connected by marriage."

"Then relationship in the twentieth century is not considered to confer prescriptive rights over the time, tastes, and associates of those connected with us?"

"Certainly not; but, within these limits the family bond is real and affectionate. To read old books, one would believe the mother-in-law was a Gorgon. You may see how much respectful consideration my husband pays to my mother, and how she regards his opinions, and admires his abilities."

We dined together at a restaurant in town, near the University, and thus missed dinner at the Owen Home. When I returned I found Mrs. Carmichael had found something among her possessions that she was sure would interest me. It was an old copy of Children of Gibeon which had belonged to her grand-mother, and had on the fly-leaf--

CHAPTER IV

88

FLORENCE HENDERSON. (From her Aunt), EMILY BETHEL.

and the date of the birthday, which was the last of hers, I could see.

"Have you read it?" I asked eagerly.

"Yes, long ago. I thought it interesting, but so strange. I have been glancing through it again to-day. The book has a special interest to us, as the author took so large a part in the founding of the People's Palace, and also, I think, had sound views on the population question." Here my kinswoman showed a little confusion of ideas.

"With your Associated Homes you are not so much in need of the Palace, which was such a desideratum when Besant wrote this book and *All Sorts and Conditions of Men*--in which his impossible hero and heroine build a Palace of delight in the East End."

"Oh, it served a good purpose, then, and continues to do so. In the neighborhood of the Palace were the first Workmen's Associated Homes, built much more cheaply than those you have seen, because they did not need such large public rooms, or so many of them. This gave the artisan and laboring class an introduction to the benefits of associated living. You will still find that near such large public Palaces--as they are called--the poorest of the people congregated, and in all large towns there are still social and musical centres, as well as educational; for in these are held the evening continuation schools, which form the main link between the common school and the university. There are few of our young people who do not try to carry their instruction further in their leisure, even though they do not care to go to the university."

"But the Melindas, and Lizzies, and Lotties of to-day; what is their condition?"

"If you can spare an hour, this afternoon, you can go with me to see them in the flesh; I want to go to the co-operative needlewomen and dressmakers, in the next street, to pay for the new dress I got for Florrie's wedding. You will see rosy cheeks and bright eyes, and happy marriages, instead of the semi-starvation and the terrible temptations

CHAPTER IV

of the *régime* of elevenpence half-penny, or what Mr. Besant calls 'the minimum day's wage on which women could subsist.'"

"Do people not make their own clothes now?"

"Many prefer to do it; I always make my own underclothes, or part of them; but I like to give out my dresses, and the dear friend whom we expect home to night--whom Mr. Oliphant calls St. Bridget--makes my bonnets and caps."

"Do your co-operative workers give hand or machine work?"

"Machine, of course, when the work is paid for; no one could afford to give the value of hand work."

"I suppose then that the typical Irish hand-made night dress--with a hundred tucks, and yards on yards of stitching and feather-stitching and embroidery let in for two shillings and twopence (a clever girl, working long hours, managing two weekly)--is a thing altogether of the past."

"Altogether exploded," said Mrs. Carmichael, laughing, "Our people don't work long hours, and not for your four-and-fourpence a week. My underclothes are all machine-made, and made to last; girls, in their leisure often put special work in their own clothes, especially for a trousseau, which is as often made after marriage as before it; but Florrie has used her leisure otherwise, and her engagement has been very short, so her father and mother gave her her clothes, which have been made at the same place as my gown--which you see is very simple, as we could not afford to pay for the machining and trimming of such a dress as you wear, for you say your crape is expensive and perishable. It would take four women two or three days to make it; mine, as you see it, can be made by machine in equal to a day and a quarter of one woman's work."

When we reached the co-operative workrooms, I found that machinery had taken more and more into its iron hands since my time, and what a wonderful six hours' work could be turned out. At this establishment they worked in two re-lays, one set beginning at seven and working till

CHAPTER IV

one, the other beginning at one and working till seven. Melinda, Lizzie, and Lottie, too, so long as her health permitted, worked from daylight till nine or ten and then sallied forth into the lighted streets, where alone they could see the life and stir of the world, could meet their friends and their lovers--resist or yield to temptations which beset those who have only the streets at night for their sole recreation ground. I could see a Melinda in the girl with the firm jaw, the resolute eyes, and the slightly disdainful carriage, sitting at a machine. "Was she married?" "No! but about to be." "Could she tell me what she did with her leisure?" "Oh yes! she made her own clothes, and those of her mother and grandmother. She had no sister, but two brothers--one of them was an enthusiastic naturalist, and she went excursions with him, and helped with his collections. She also had a taste herself for physiology, and attended the lectures on that subject at the People's Palace." There was one like Lizzie, with lovely eyes and a yielding expression, but a better-fed, better-clothed and better-taught Lizzie. She had married at sixteen--which was too early, even for the twentieth century--a lad of eighteen, and had not got on well with her husband; incompatibility of temper, and general discordance of tastes led to a divorce--after sufficient time given to consider the step--and she had married again an older man, with whom she seemed very happy. Here, too, was a Lottie--at least she had a pale face and a weak back, so that she could not work the sewing machine, but she had great taste in designing new styles, and in trimming; she lived in the same Home as the other two girls, in which she had every comfort, and her day's work was not too much for her. The three girls seemed to be good friends, but were not so absolutely dependent on each other as in the times when they had to club together to pay the rent for a single room, and sleep together in the same bed. Opportunities for heroic self-sacrifice were no longer open to the exceptionally generous, but opportunities of neighborly kindness, and sharing of thoughts and ideas were still given.

I noticed that the trousseau which Florence Oliphant received from her parents--though she was satisfied and delighted with it--compared very poorly with what her ancestress, my Florrie, got in 1886. It was neither so abundant nor so elaborate. Belle's fad for hand-made underlinen, her love of the best article, her appreciation of the finest of embroidery and of lace--as well as her general desire to eclipse the trousseau of a certain Miss Jones Smith--had loaded Florrie's trunks and lightened her father's pocket. I fear Belle would have looked on the modest belongings of her descendant as the outfit of a housemaid--and not very smart at that; not a scrap of real lace, but a pretty veil and bonnet of machine lace. Such a thing as a bridal veil of fine Brussels lace, which cost £500 two years' back, and the worker's eyesight, was relegated to the Dark Ages. As for Mrs. Carmichael's simple grey dress, it was slightly modified from her husband's original design, as years advanced. The cap was St. Bridget's masterpiece, so that, as Florrie said, "Grandmother would look so lovely at the wedding that nobody would look at herself, but perhaps Fred, a little."

CHAPTER V

THURSDAY

Marriage and the Relations of the Sexes

This was the day fixed for the marriage of my very great grand-niece Florence Oliphant to Frederick Steele, and I was glad to see that with all the changes made by a century of revolution, most people, including my own kindred, still looked on marriage as a religious ceremony, and had it performed by a clergyman, or by what might be called a clergywoman--for the clerical profession had opened its gates to women. The officiating minister was the lady whom Mr. Oliphant called St. Bridget, and a most impressive ceremony she made it. She knew both the bridegroom and the bride well. Many marriages still took place in Church, but this was performed in the house which had been that of the bride's family for so many generations. Several friends and kinsfolk were invited to whom I was introduced as a relative from Adelaide; there was no need to let my extraordinary story run the gauntlet of more than Mrs. Carmichael and the Oliphants, to whom I was therefore obliged to keep close, lest my ignorance and absurd questions should betray me. There were also a good many members of the Owen Home present by invitation.

Although the ceremony was religious it was not indissoluble. The fervent prayer for constancy, which closed the service, showed that this was a thing which might or might not follow the vows, which were more like aspirations than oaths. The early marriages, which were all but universal in the society of the twentieth century, demanded a much less stringent bond than either the Catholic or Protestant Church in our times would permit. Young, unproved boys and girls became attached to each other, desired to be companions for life, and afterwards found they had made a mistake--as was the case with the pretty girl I called Lizzie, at the Co-operative Dressmaking establishment. Marriage was considered to be a matter which should be perfectly free for young people to engage in, according to liking or even caprice.

The evils of checking early marriages had been felt to be too great, too destructive to virtue, to health, and to happiness for any considerations of prudence or ambition to stand in the way. Parents, indeed, warned against excessively early unions, and public opinion (here, as in other things, the collective conscience) discouraged marriages under the age of nineteen for lads, and seventeen for girls. But though marriage, even earlier, was free and quite legal, parenthood was never allowed till the young people were in the full vigor of manhood and womanhood. Science has put it into the power of the married people to regulate their families, and it was considered disgraceful not only to have too many children, but to bring into the world the progeny of the immature or the sickly. Until the bride and bridegroom, whose marriage I witnessed, were able to maintain themselves and to provide for children, they would remain childless. The parents, on both sides, continued to maintain them, and to carry their professional education to its conclusion; but they were spared the responsibilities of a family.

Mr. Oliphant did not give the bride away, as in our time. The young people gave themselves to each other. It was evidently looked upon as their own affair; they did not actually promise and vow to love, honor, and cherish each other, but only to try to do these things; the vow of obedience was left out. I recollect, so well, Jeannie's Bethel saying to me--it was with regard to her sister Florrie, who found it so hard to obey her husband, when she saw his real character--"It is not the obedience that is so hard, auntie; if Florrie could love and honor him, it would be easy to obey; obedience is the least part of it!" I thought it a very clever remark on Jeannie's part.

These early marriages entered into with faith in the future, but not making too heavy a pull on the present, relieved society from the incubus of wedding presents, which I have always thought a tax levied in inverse proportion to need, for the richer the couple were, the handsomer the gifts were bound to be. There was no wedding breakfast, though the guests all partook of a meal with the rest of the families, and with the bride and bridegroom, who, after it, got on to a tricycle and went down to the seaside at a quiet place to spend the time till Monday, when they would return to take up their quarters together in the Owen Home, and continue their studies as if nothing had happened. They had both heard lectures that morning, and chose this time, because Friday happened to be a light day, and they thought they might have one holiday.

CHAPTER V

How much less expense and trouble and worry there seemed to be for all parties concerned when marriage was the common natural event of one's teens, and not, as with too many, "the dim far-off event" that never came at all, or came late in life, after many hopes and disappointments. Although interesting to the young people and to their affectionate parents, a marriage was no longer a great or fashionable affair, with lawyers drawing up settlements, milliners and dressmakers and needlewomen making mountains of clothes, houses to buy or to rent, furniture to choose, and cards and cake to be sent to the chosen circle of friends and acquaintances, and presents to receive from the liberal or the conventional. There was not now any chance of the celibacy that stared so many single women in the face when there were a million in England who could not be married unless Mormon ideas prevailed. Population had not only been kept stationary, but the sexes had been equalised.

So long as there were no children born of a marriage, divorce was easily obtained. A declaration by both parties that they sought release, repeated after three months given for reconsideration, was sufficient. After children were born, matters became more serious and difficult, this required three declarations, extending over twelve months. The nearest relatives on both sides were chosen as arbiters of the guardianship of the child or children. When divorce was sought by one party and not by the other, which was comparatively rare, the complainant was at a disadvantage with regard to the children, and this was frequently a cause of re-union, for the love of children was exceedingly strong, and it was possible for either man or woman to bring up the small family. The divorces were published, as I had seen, in the ordinary newspapers, after the marriages, and one month after divorce the parties might marry again. It was generally as easy for the woman to marry again as the man, especially when the family of two was divided, one to each. When there were three, though the odd child could not be halved, the parents shared the cost of maintenance.

I was afraid to ask the proportion of divorces to marriages. It was large, but not so large as I feared, and much larger in the youthful and childless stages than afterwards.

"But you have many divorces," I said.

CHAPTER V

"It is not given to everyone to be constant," said Mrs. Oliphant, "even public opinion, which discountenances many marriages and many divorces, cannot control everyone. But constancy is on the whole a stronger principle with the bulk of our race than the love of change, and all our institutions foster it. For my own part I have a tolerably firm belief that Florrie and Fred Steele will go on pulling together as happily as her father and I have done, and as her grandmother did before us with the dear old grandfather. Florrie is a good, true-hearted girl, and her little ambitions are such as Fred will aid and not discourage. This is, of course, as far as I can see; but if he were to change, if we were all mistaken in his character, so that misery and not happiness were the result of their union, then we have the resource of separation, and a chance of better things for Florrie with another."

"Divorce is not disgraceful or discreditable now-a-days, then? The proceedings in the Divorce Court used to be the most sickening of reading."

"Ah, true!" said Mrs. Oliphant, "because it was only granted for one cause, and that was difficult of proof, and in the search for evidence much dirty linen was washed in public; but now, owing to the easiness of procuring divorce, that cause is comparatively rare. Fidelity to the marriage bond, while it lasts, seems to be a point of honor with people who can sever it on reasonable grounds."

"I have often felt the need of relaxation of the strongest marriage vows in especial cases, but yet this seems undue laxity. I see, too, great dangers to the permanence of your early marriages, before young people rightly know their own mind, in your living together in associated homes. Florrie may see and become intimately acquainted with someone who pleases her better than her husband; Fred might be captivated by another woman. There appears no restful finality in your matrimonial bond."

"Does it really strike you in that way? We are used to the contingencies through habit."

"Jealousy might be so easily awakened, and so hard to lull to sleep, or do you consider jealousy one of the primitive passions that were

CHAPTER V
96

necessary for the evolution of the race from the community of wives and husbands which made the social unit, the family, an impossibility? On jealousy, I suppose, has been built monogamy, the one husband of one wife, which, with a little latitude for change, is still your social order."

"Jealousy, as it was felt long ago between husband and wife, has been much modified and softened," said Mrs. Oliphant. "Did not the pictures of savage jealousy and revenge in Shakespeare and the older dramatists, such as are given in Othello and the Winter's Tale, shock even your generation?"

"Yes," I said, "especially the younger among us."

"And even in your day, it was possible for a husband warmly attached to his wife to enjoy friendship of a very tender kind with other women--her friends and companions, or his own old friends--and for a married woman keenly to enjoy the society and the deference of an intelligent and agreeable man not her husband, without either party taking umbrage at it?"

"That depends so much on the disposition," I said. "Some men and some women would be jealous of shadows. Even where the coarser form of jealousy is absent there always has been, and I thought there always would be, a certain exclusiveness about married love, and a sense of the paramount claim which husband and wife have over each other. The things you speak of were pleasant, no doubt, but they had in them more or less of danger."

"Yes, especially in an idle society, or in a society where the husband was absorbed in business, and furnished the means for his wife to be extravagant and luxurious as well as idle. Too engrossed with money-making to spare time to be agreeable to her, or to keep his hold on her heart by letting her share his cares, he might think he satisfied all her claims, reasonable and unreasonable, with his cheque-book. In our busy hives there is neither overwork for the many, or that plethora of leisure for the wealthy, or the out-of-work periods for the poorer classes, which led to the vice and crime of old society. Everyone works and works with the whole heart for a large portion of the day, and this

CHAPTER V

gives us relish for the leisure which is allowed to everyone in the same proportion."

"But there are many instances of change of affection in your twentieth century marriages."

"I do not deny it, but on the whole we think happiness is promoted by making the marriage tie reasonably elastic."

"All your arrangements seem to be brought to the test of happiness. The old Benthamite principle, the greatest happiness of the greatest number, seems to decide everything with you."

"Well," said Mrs. Oliphant calmly, "can you suggest any better test?"

"It would be despised by saints and ascetics."

"Hear St. Bridget on this subject. Saints despise their own happiness, but not that of other people, and as for asceticism even she has given that up. And as to St. Bridget herself, she is an instance in point about the jealousy you think so dangerous. No man can love his wife more than my husband loves me, but yet there are points in his spiritual nature that are touched by our dear old maid as I cannot touch them. He delights in her society. He quotes her sayings, he has taken her advice--especially about the children--but I am not jealous. I have professional relations and warm friendships with the other sex, and especially with one old schoolfellow settled here in the Owen Home, but I am sure it never occurred to Arthur to be jealous."

"I am not naturally jealous myself," said I, "I always thought that my friends loved me as much as I deserved, and as much as I could make them love me, but then there was no lover and no husband in my case, and I have always been told that while human nature continued to be human nature, jealousy must be the watchful guardian of love."

"Well, one reason of our feeling of security may be that we live so much in public in our Associated Homes, and are so much in the habit of seeking out our affinities openly, that intrigue has little, if any, place in our lives. When a separation of married people is imminent there is

CHAPTER V

generally another preference on one side, rarely on both, but the matter is openly and candidly handled."

"You think then that secrecy, intrigue, and the idea that there was the excitement of wrong doing, led to our old divorce court suits, which I confess were a scandal among a moral and civilised people. You may never have heard of the Frenchman who had been in the habit of spending all his spare time with a certain madame, a widow, charming and lively, and when his own wife died and he thought of a successor, being recommended to marry this fascinating lady, protesting that it was impossible, for in that case where could he spend his evenings?"

"Here, if we spend our evenings with an affinity our husband or wife can follow us and make one of the group. At least in the Home, where you consider the element of danger is strongest."

"It certainly was in the countries where divorce was impossible that marital relations were most unsatisfactory. The disgraceful *menage-à-trois* which was so common among the higher ranks in France, could not have existed if the bond could have been broken. Just as I left the world divorce was allowed by the State in France, though not by the Church. There must have been license at first, I feel sure."

"Yes, there was, but we have settled down."

"But what say the churches, especially the Catholic Church, which, I understand, still exists?"

"The churches have developed a marvellous faculty of adaptation, and by so doing have prevented their own extinction. Even the Catholic Church has been made to feel that the interests of humanity as interpreted by common sense and experience are paramount. Of course it still claims infallibility but it had shifted ground even in your day, and has shifted much more since. The socialism which was a greater terror to her than heresy and Protestantism, she has been obliged to accept, in order that she may keep hold of her people. She has had to lose her temporalities and work like other churches of the day, and as to marriage she would lose all hold on society if she

CHAPTER V

refused to marry divorced people."

"This is all so new to me that I need to take breath over it," said I. "I acknowledge that our old marriage system had many failures, and that holding parties to a bond of the most intimate personal relations after all the love and honor had died out, was, in many cases, very cruel."

"It was not only cruel, it was degrading and demoralising," said Mrs. Oliphant. "Those who love each other feel the bond to be final and rest in it. Those who do not love each other are not compelled to drag a chain. We have got used to our system, and find it works well in most cases, while it has put an end, as nothing else could have done, to the foulest spot in your old civilisation--mercenary love, and to the one-sided arrangement by which a man could (as it was called) protect a woman one day, and turn her adrift the next, with a stigma on her character which prevented her from forming an honorable union, while he might be sought by mothers for their innocent daughters."

"And you have really put an end to venal love and to temporary *liaisons*?"

"Yes. Every woman can be married. She will not give herself for anything less honorable. When love exists, human nature desires permanent union. You know, Miss Bethel, it is the love that sanctifies the marriage rather than the marriage that sanctifies the love."

"Yes; perhaps that is the right way to look on it. And, of course, anything that could grapple successfully with what you rightly call the plague spot of civilisation, may have some slight drawbacks, and yet be a mighty boon to humanity."

"You cannot tell how much health has improved after about three generations of early marriages. Another point that makes such youthful unions easy and desirable is that there is no uncertain quantity in the way of family to be provided for. I suppose you have seen families of twelve and more?"

"Oh, yes. An ancestress of mine and, of course, of yours, had twenty-one children. If she heard of any family smaller, she thought

CHAPTER V

nothing of it; if she heard of any larger, she did not believe it. My father used to visit in his young days two of her children, who were his great aunts--two out of a set of triplets, who, all three, lived till they were eighteen, and the two survivors to a great age."

"Well, was there anything remarkable about them, except their belonging to so large a family?" said Mrs. Oliphant rather cynically.

"Not that I know of. It was not the dominant strain in the blood of the Bethels. But," continued I, "quoting from the last book I read (before Scientific Meliorism, one of the Eminent Women series), Susannah Wesley was the twenty-fifth child of her father (by his second wife, certainly), and she bore to her husband--a poor clergyman in Lincolnshire--no less than 19 children, of whom John, the founder of Methodism, was the sixteenth, and Charles, the sweet singer of the connexion, was the eighteenth. Under your *régime* these great English revivalists would never have been born, and England would have missed much. Sir Isaac Newton, too, was so sickly when born that the Spartans would have given him his quietus, and, I suppose, so should you; you object to delicate children, I understand?"

"No; except when there is idiocy, we preserve, by all means in our power, the most delicate children, and often find they have rare gifts. We object to delicate adults becoming parents, but where life is, we try to make the most and the best of it. My mother tells me you were interested in Eveline Smith, whom you called Lottie. That girl cost me a great deal of thought and care, but she has repaid it, for not only has she special talent in the higher branch of her trade, but she has a wonderful voice for singing."

"But the Wesleys?"

"I give up the Wesleys; but I certainly think that we have a greater chance of capacity, and even genius, from members of small families all in sound health and carefully brought up--not dragged up, as so many of your large families were."

"I am not so sure of the genius," said I. "The average may be high, but the exceptions may be less striking and less useful."

CHAPTER V

"I cannot, of course, be sure. To the great ones who led the van of civilisation, and especially to those who might be called the forlorn hope, through persecution, through dense stupidity, through misrepresentation, we are fully sensible of our infinite obligations. Life is so much easier now that there appears less to do, but the good and wise are always doing something. I think the world is better since I first knew it, and that is a cheerful thought."

"But, in marrying your daughter, you do not get her off your hands," said I, recurring to the old subject.

"No, not for some years, even pecuniarily. We continue to maintain Florence till she is fitted to take the position she aims at; and Fred's parents do the same by him. I don't want to get my only girl off my hands, by any means, and I was glad she chose the Owen Home instead of Mrs. Steele's, at the Evergreen."

"But is there room at these homes for married people to settle down where they please?"

"Florrie only moves from a small room to a larger one--exchanging with a widow whose husband died lately, and who wished the small room. The homes are fairly elastic. They could have managed at the Evergreen for all they need for the present. You see, the young people cost us no more than they did, and they are happier; they work more earnestly. You cannot think how restful to the brain and to the nerves an early, happy marriage is."

"I suppose it is so; more than the long engagement which was the only spur in my time, but which had its uncertainties, its jealousies, its discouragements. Loving mothers have assured me that they objected to the wearing nature of a long, or uncertain, engagement for their daughters; prudent fathers considered it a clog on their sons, and, yet I have seen instances in which it was like salvation to both parties."

"Fred and his wife, you see, need no costly furnishing. They take no wedding trip. Florrie's *trousseau* is made to last. We don't expect to have much to buy for her for the next two years or more, so it comes to the same thing, and the girl rejoices in her new clothes."

CHAPTER V

"It used to be thought very dangerous for young married people to take up their abode in their parents' house, but I observe that it is very frequent with you. Most families in the Owen Home seem to have three generations--though, of course, there is not room for all of your descendants."

"Sometimes people are bought out to make room, but, as a rule, we object to selling our home. But, with a stationary population, we can accommodate each other generally. Either the husband or the wife finds a corner in a parent nest."

"How do you avoid the friction which was all but universal in joint households among English and American people? The French managed it better. Economy dictated the common homes; but I used to think they agreed better because they lived more out of doors than the Anglo-Saxon, and the proverbially small French family might also have helped."

"Possibly so; but I dare say the French people were more accommodating. What did your contemporaries quarrel about when they attempted to live together?"

"Housekeeping, very frequently. The older generation thought the younger lavish and thoughtless; the younger thought the older prejudiced and stingy."

"Well, the housekeeping is done for us, so that element of discord is absent."

"They differed often as to the choice of society. Sometimes the older generation were slaves to Mrs. Grundy (if you ever heard of that potentate) and saw advantages in cultivating the acquaintance of rich or titled, but dull and tiresome people, while the young folks liked those who were more frivolous and amusing. On the other hand, the young used to class as old fogies and bores many excellent, and sensible, and intelligent old family friends and relatives. People of different ages naturally chose different friends."

"Here we, as a rule, are most intimate with the inhabitants of our own Home, though others are open to us, where we may go as guests and visitors. Among a community which averages more than a hundred, there are generally to be found those who suit each other, and as the young people have been brought up together, and the older people have grown old together, they are likely to form strong friendships in the home. We are accustomed to choose the society we prefer, and to be civil and polite to those we are more indifferent to. So this cause of friction is reduced in proportions by our arrangements."

"Then, though the gentlemen might have agreed fairly well, only seeing each other after business hours, the women who had to stay at home all day, could rarely stand the strain."

"Well, our women have their work, generally out of doors, like men, which makes this danger the less."

"The Germans used to have a proverb that a man could live happily with his wife's mother (the *bête noir* of English and American Satirists), but that no woman could live amicably with her husband's mother, whom she could never escape from, whose Argus eyes discovered all her short-comings, and saw slights to herself, and neglects or injuries to her son when none was intended; but the strain in your Associated Homes must be much slighter. The mother-in-law can find congenial society with people of her own age, and knit and gossip to her heart's content, and leave her daughter-in-law to follow out her own life. But, I believe that servants were another fruitful cause of quarrel as well as an unfailing subject for gossip and tattle. You can surely still talk about your attendants."

"Yes, but we cannot dismiss them at our own caprice; all complaints must be made to the home committee, both by the inhabitants of the home and by the attendants."

"And they cannot leave you in the lurch on the approach of the Christmas holiday, or just on the eve of a dinner party, as I have seen over and over again in Australia?"

CHAPTER V

"No, the arrangement holds good for a year and is generally renewed. Each attendant has a right to certain holidays. We cannot possibly quarrel about servants."

"But you may about children. Is no devoted mother convinced that her darling gets less than his or her share of attention from the nurses? The common nursery would, in my day, have been a common battle ground. Even the most reasonable of women seemed to lose her balance where her children were concerned."

"All I can say is that I suppose our mothers have become accustomed to the system, and the devoted mothers have more of their children's society than those who are more philosophical."

"I dare say the large numbers and the noisiness of the young Britons and the young Americans, were hard on the old people when there was joint-housekeeping, without extensive nursery arrangements."

"I dare say they were. Mr. Oliphant gave me to read, as a curiosity, an old book he had picked up, called 'Helen's Babies.' Of course it was satire, but it must have had some foundation. How intolerable the American child of a century back must have been!"

"Perhaps one cause of friction with us was divided authority--the noise of children was hard on the nerves and temper of old folks; they were apt to be irritated but not firm, and the grandparents would concede what the parents forbade. John Wesley said his mother--though the firmest and wisest of Autocrats with her own large family whom she taught and trained with Spartan rigor--spoiled her grandchildren."

"Probably she was worn out with her hard life, and was glad to be indulgent when she had no responsibility. I cannot recollect of any trouble in this way. Florrie and her elder brothers Jack and Everard, were a great pleasure and resource to their grandmother, and to my father while he lived."

"And you have lived without a quarrel, without a difference?"

"Not without a difference, but certainly without a quarrel."

CHAPTER V

"Do you hope to make room for your younger son, Everard, when he returns from his travels and chooses a wife for himself, and goes, as you intend him to do, into his father's office?"

"Everard is still on our books as an inmate, and we should like very much to keep him, for Mr. Oliphant would like to have Everard always at his side in his hobbies as well as in the office work, especially the "History of Co-operation;" but, of course, it will depend upon what the young lady likes."

"You have no idea of his keeping single. I suppose you have very few old maids or bachelors now-a-days?"

"Very few indeed. I have a pretty large acquaintance, but I could count the number of unmarried people over twenty-five years old on the fingers of one hand. We are quite proud of Miss Somerville, 'St. Bridget' as my husband calls her, because she is that exceptional person--an old maid. She seems to belong to all of us in the Home, because she has not given herself to any husband; not but that she has had many offers, but her vocation, she says, is for single life and general motherhood. In old days she would have been a tender mystic and, probably, a dedicated nun."

"She has been born out of due time then?"

"I do not think so. There can never be a state of society which is not the better for saintly souls."

"But what is there left for these saintly souls to do? I feel puzzled to think what I, Emily Bethel, with the wisdom and the experience of my sixty-two years, could find to employ me in this world of yours. I should miss the charitable and philanthrophic work that occupied so much of my time and my thoughts before my mother's failing health made such exclusive demands on me. Nobody now is called on to furnish doctor, and nurse, and baby linen to the impecunious many-childed--nobody is needed to go district visiting to bestow advice and charity, and to keep eyes and ears open to detect imposition. Not only the Union Workhouse, but the Benevolent Asylum is shut up. There are no longer State children to find homes for, or to visit in these homes. There is no

CHAPTER V

crêche to establish and superintend; there are no fallen girls to attempt to rescue, and even in the more hopeful work of prevention there is nothing to do. The Girls' Friendly Society is without an object. Penny clubs and clothing clubs are, of course, extinct. Even in prosperous Australia, the number of voluntary benevolent associations was large, and continually increasing. I used to help with money and personal service in many such organisations, and was requested to help in as many more."

"In fact all the old patronage of the poor is abolished," said Mrs. Oliphant. "It was because of ignorance, neglect and vice being so prevalent that the army of philanthropic workers were called out to spend and be spent in the service of humanity, and their endeavors seemed to exonerate the mass of mankind from doing anything at all."

"There were those who gave cheques and those who gave service, and some who gave both, but an immense number gave nothing--scarcely good will," said I, "and I confess that I often felt that our well-meant efforts sapped the spirit of self-respect and independence among my poorer brothers, and especially among the women."

"A laborer's wife would now-a-days be insulted by the offer of baby-linen, or of old clothes," said Mrs. Oliphant. "The common contribution to her Associated Home covers her medical expenses, and if she cannot afford to pay a nurse, there are members of the home who attend on her, she being willing to take her share with others. The common nursery, for which she pays the full value, answers for a *crêche* when she has to leave her young children to earn her livelihood. All the comforts which in old times were so difficult to purchase for herself, and which there was a demoralising chance that other people might bestow on her, are now taken into her reckoning of necessary expenses."

"Then I go back to my old question:--What would there be for such a woman as me to do beyond supplying my own necessities and taking my own pleasure? It seems to set life on a lower level."

CHAPTER V

"We can help our fellows in many ways still. Miss Somerville is a born religious teacher, and she works at our continuation schools, and with our little ones at the Owen Home, endeavouring to add to the excellent secular influences which go to form character, a spiritual motive, and a lofty ideal."

"What is her avocation? Oh, I forgot, she is a clergywoman."

"Oh, don't you know she is a milliner, especially clever in styles for the middle-aged and old. The other calling, of course, brings in no income."

"Indeed, this is a very voluntary sort of church. Caps and bonnets seem rather frivolous concerns to occupy the working hours of a religious genius."

"Do you think so?" said my kinswoman. "So long as people wear caps and bonnets, it is worthwhile to make them becoming and suitable to age. I think the bread earning employment keeps our religious teachers healthy in mind and body."

"I thought," said I, hesitatingly, "that this was a middle-class home, representing the educated and professional classes, but I heard Mr. Black to-day talk of the foundry at which he works, and Mrs. Roberts told me she was a bookbinder, and here you say Miss Somerville is a milliner!"

"We were originally a middle-class home," said Mrs. Oliphant; "but people cannot keep up the old proportion of distributors and soft-handed clerks. Every child who comes out of our schools is fitted to be a clerk--but the market is limited. Quite half of the inhabitants of the Owen Home are engaged in work which would have been considered *infra dig.* by their great-grand parents. We have still some of the possessions and the traditions of a time when we had material and mental superiority. If Florrie had not had a love of books and a taste for teaching, she would probably have learned millinery from Miss Somerville, of whom she is fond. By-the-by, it may interest you to know that she is a descendant of the Mrs. Somerville who was an eminent person in your day."

CHAPTER V

"Yes, her life was a favorite book with my mother, who, though she did not know her, knew the Somervilles well. Her honorable life and her serene, cheerful old age, occupied and interested to the last, were pleasant to read of, and to think of."

I had a peep at the room prepared for the young people on their return. A friend of the bridegroom's--a clever mechanic--had made a special writing-table, at which two could work together. Some of the furniture was new, but most of it was old. As old pillow lace was only held as heirlooms, and valued highly, I made a gift of a piece of handsome lace which had been my mother's, which had somehow found its way into my bag, for the bride to receive on her return.

There had been little of what we would call romance in the courtship and marriage. The young people did not require much, and the parents were reasonable and kind. The great charm in the match was that they were fellow-students, but that was too common to be specially held up for felicitations. It was simply the natural order of things that two young people should prefer each other to all the world beside, and with the least possible delay, convert their dream of love into a reality. Dear me! where was the chance for the novel writer of the nineteenth century, when would he find a love situation interesting enough to keep his readers awake for half the night, as has happened to me many a time both in my youth and my middle age?

I glanced at the little shelf of books which were specially Florrie's own; they were mostly books for study. Her light literature was obtained from the Owen Home library, but there were two volumes of poetry presented by Fred, with evident marks of reading, a novel written by an aunt, which was a presentation copy, and another which Florrie had bought with her own pocket-money. I was living so intensely that I could not find time for reading, and the little I read seemed much more unreal than the conversation, but I felt I ought to go and overhaul the books in the Owen Home, and see how many of our old standard books had a place on the permanent staff. I was disappointed to find how few books, that I had thought were written for all time, were to be seen there. Of course, in the British Museum and at the great public libraries which existed in all large towns, I could find my old favorites, but the ordinary daily reading of the people of the twentieth century was the more recent work of contemporaries.

As I stood reading the titles of the books on the shelves, and occasionally opening one, Mrs. Oliphant joined me and recommended one especially to me as giving a history of the Industrial and Social Revolution, and another of earlier date as the most powerful book written on behalf of the relaxation of the marriage laws, and the limitation of families.

"I cannot read," I said--at least nothing at all demanding thought or study. "This week is so short, I must get my information made as easy as possible. I may glance at Florrie's favorite novel and her favorite poems, but I fear I could not read even your great history of co-operation in my present condition of mind."

"I can quite understand that reading is all but impossible to you."

"I am very troublesome to you with my questions, but I dare not ask other people, lest I should show my ignorance of things here, and I fear to be questioned about the Australia of to-day, because I would show quite as great ignorance of things there. But the permanence of your homes, the way they descend to new pairs, makes me think what a terrible collapse there must have been in all the building trades, after the *furore* there must have been before the building of Associated Homes. Were many of the old houses available?

"A good many churches and public buildings were remodelled and enlarged, and often the nucleus was old, but the best and most convenient were those which were planned from foundation to attics for twenty or more families, like this Owen Home. The Ossulton Home, which you saw, is newer, but not more comfortable, and, of course, not so much beautified. Fred leaves a beautiful home, the Evergreen. There have been several generations of artists in that home, who always leave traces of their presence, and he tells me the lawn is better than ours."

"But, to return to my puzzle," I said, "there must have been a period of inflation in the building trades, when homes were thus reconstructed, as well as a prodigious loss of property when the old homes were abandoned."

"Yes, of course, there was loss. The general gain was at the cost of enormous individual losses. Millionaires found a shrinkage in values unprecedented in the severest crisis or panic before. Territorial magnates, especially ground landlords, and owners of houses, freehold or leasehold, were ruined by the thousands and tens of thousands. But, somehow, nobody starved."

"Then, when the Associated Homes were all built and tenanted, and England--or the old three kingdoms, as I knew them--made less population by the emigration of a sixth part of their inhabitants, and the population kept thereafter rigidly stationary, what could there be for the members of the building trade to do?"

"It is a reasonable question. We had had, however, before that, stood the still greater strain of absorbing the armies of the country and all those who lived by the manufacture of arms, ammunition, and accoutrements--all who depended directly or indirectly on the two great arms of the service by land and sea--into the ranks of productive labor. Many of them swelled the building trades, and housed themselves and others. Many of the co-operative artisans' houses were built by the future inhabitants--each putting so much labor to reduce the original cost--and many excellent ideas were evolved by people building for their own comfort and convenience."

"But, when the houses were built and tenanted, what did the masons, and carpenters, and plasterers, and half of the painters, and paper-hangers find to do?"

"Everybody has a bye-trade, besides the one followed for a livelihood."

"In my experience, when trade was dull in one line, it was generally dull in all lines; but then, we had such alternations of inflation and depression. Things are steadier with you."

"The builders, generally, took to cultivation, and large tracts of inferior land were utilised. A number were kept on for repairs, and the adapted and remodelled old homes needed a great deal of this. But, of course,

CHAPTER V

there was an immense displacement of labor, though not so much as there was in England and the Continent, where general disarming took place."

"I suppose war was put an end to because the burden of taxation was no longer endurable?'

"Partly so; but quite as much because engines were devised and constructed so destructive that human nature recoiled from them in horror. England, France and Germany were the pioneers in substituting arbitration for war, Austria and Italy followed close, and the pressure of the Great Powers was too much for the brute force of Russia, which was besides honey-combed by the anti-warlike doctrines of Socialists and Nihilists. The less powerful nations, of course, formed a compact phalanx in favor of peace."

"The saving to the nations of the world by the cessation of war, and of the ever-enlarging preparations to be made in case of the sudden outbreak of war must have been immense, though of course, the crisis must have been acute. Does this nation increase in wealth while the population remains stationary? We used to think wealth expanded with the number of workers."

"At least the value of property did, measured in money," said Mr. Oliphant, smiling severely. "The average income or earnings of the people have increased; the average capital or saved earnings may not be so great in the aggregate. Everyone has savings for old age, but very few have much more than is needed."

"If three or four generations are as saving as I have known them to be, there must be people who are rich?"

"Parsimony of this kind rarely lasts so long in a family, but we have one instance of it in the Owen Home. Mr. Harrop is the descendant of four generations of economists." "What does he do with his capital?"

"Lends it at two per cent. on excellent security, either on houses or on industrial or agricultural concerns. Cheap money has been the chief factor in reclaiming indifferent land."

CHAPTER V

"Cheap capital and costly labor," said I. "In the colonies we had to work with both at high rates."

"But your land was cheap enough," said Mr. Oliphant. "The curse of England in your old days was that capital flowed freely for all sorts of speculative ventures all over the world, but not freely for industrial purposes. The competition of all the world brought such a fall in prices that legitimate industry was paralysed."

"No doubt," said I, "in our time there was enormous wealth, enormous waste, and enormous want."

"Three portentous capital W's, owing to the withdrawal of capital from its right uses. Now, you will note, we have to eat our own broken victuals, or feed our domestic animals with them; we wear out our own clothes, or make them down for our own children. There are no beggars at our gates desiring to be fed with the crumbs that fall from the rich man's table, or to be clothed with the unsuitable garments of which fashion had grown weary. Neither have we irresponsible and pampered menials wasting what might have fed poor families. We not only save the waste of war, almost all the waste of litigation, the waste of leakage in the raising and disbursing the taxation for the expenses of Government, but we save the personal waste which was so enormous in the days of individualism and unrestricted competition."

"But you say that the average income is greater than it used to be for the larger population, when the millionaires were included. There were miles and miles of streets in London and other large cities that could only be inhabited by people spending from five to thirty-thousand a year."

"Yes, the average income is higher, and the average of good food, clothes, lodging, leisure, and amusement, which the income can buy, is also higher--and that is the true test of an income. The rich man could not eat the share of a hundred, or the rich woman wear more than one set of garments at a time, and, so, ninety-nine had less than was good or pleasant for them, that the hundredth might waste the more."

CHAPTER V

I sat in the ladies' workroom for half-an-hour in the evening. Someone was eager to teach me a new stitch in knitting, but I declined, as I had no prospect of practising it. I went early to my room to write down my day's acquisitions, so as to have a little more sleep than I had had recently.

CHAPTER VI

FRIDAY

Government and Laws

This was the day which I meant to devote to London, under the guidance of Mr. Oliphant. It was, indeed, a different London from that which I had seen in my childhood--before our family sailed for Australia--and even more different from what it had been on my visit to England in 1865-6. What losses people must have made; what fearful collapses of wealth in individuals and corporations must have taken place, in the transformation of the mart of the world into the mere capital of a small but vigorous nation! It was to me pathetic to see the diminished shipping in the Thames. No doubt other ports had a larger share of what trade remained, but the dominant fact was clear enough, that all countries in the world depended more on internal resources, and much less on foreign supplies than in the days of London's pre-eminent glory. Such countries as through their vast extent could provide for their people the produce of various latitudes, had even less foreign trade than England. Russia, and the United States, and Australia, had this wide range of climate, but even England had largely extended her list of products.

Where there had been large warehouses in the city were now co-operative stores, and many Associated Homes were made out of bonded stores and other great buildings, no longer needed for merchandise.

All my old recollections has been of London encroaching on the country, and stretching out its myriad arms, and seizing here a common, there a heath, here a sheltering wood, there a cultivated field. Now the fields and vegetable life had their innings against encroaching bricks and mortar and human swarms. Great nests of rookeries had been pulled down where population had been thickest and most wretched, and planted with trees or laid out in grass. No longer was there a street or home in London out of reach of an open space. Even little children could walk as far as to get to a park or large square, where there was fresh air to breathe and plenty of greenery to

CHAPTER VI

look on. There were new streets laid out with the homes of the period, and so broad that there was room for trees along each side of the street. The underground railway had fallen into disuse--there was plenty of space above to run all the necessary trains. Omnibuses were no more, the tramcars were no longer drawn by horses. The most fashionable part of the day no longer called out the luxurious carriages with beautiful horses and liveried servants, in which the rich and the titled had driven in Hyde Park. Nor did Rotten Row afford the sight of yore. Horses were costly luxuries which few could afford, but cycling was the favorite exercise of the young and a very useful means of locomotion for all ages.

The street traffic, of course, was enormously reduced, for London only contained as many inhabitants as it did at the beginning of this century--about a million--and to this number I learned, to my satisfaction, that Paris and New York had also been brought.

The nineteenth century was commonly spoken of as the age of great cities, the twentieth was extolled as being the age of dispersion. Provincial towns, perhaps, took more stand, as compared with London, than of old, but yet London was the seat of legislation, the centre of Government, the heart of the kingdom still. I was glad that no fancy for symmetry, no passion for decentralisation had carried the political capital out of the grand historic London. I was also pleased to see that most of the old buildings--civil and ecclesiastical--that were beautiful in themselves, or memorable in history, had been carefully preserved in their original form. The Tower, St. Paul's, Westminster Abbey, Westminster Hall, still stood as they had stood for centuries. The finest of the old churches had been preserved, though others had been reconstructed into homes.

Time fails me to tell of the surprising transformation of London. The river still flowed with all its ancient majesty, and more than its ancient purity, and there were landmarks, here and there, to convince me that this was really the great city; but the destruction of the slums and the reconstruction of the better streets made it most bewildering to me. The railway stations still stood where they were. How I regretted I could not take the Great Northern Railway and see for myself what had been done with the land of my birth.

CHAPTER VI

"Stands Scotland where it did?" I asked my patient though often somewhat amused guide.

"I believe it does," he said smiling.

"If, as you say, the wealth or prosperity of a country depends on its fertility, Scotland must be far behind England!"

"Scotland and England are one, and it is not only fertility of soil and kindliness of climate, but the ingenuity and industry of its inhabitants that bring prosperity to a country, and Scotland has these."

"And what of Ireland?" I asked.

"Ireland is still very much of a dairy and cattle-breeding country. England depends on her for much of her butter and cheese and beef supply. She grows rye and flax of better quality than we can in England, and, in some manufactures and in many handmade articles, the Irish excel us. Ireland is poor in minerals, no doubt, but the reclamation of bog land and the increase of production has been marvellous since the pacification of the country, and the flow of capital as well as of steady industry on to the land."

"There is then no bitterness left between England and Ireland? It seems too much to expect after so many centuries of misgovernment and misunderstanding."

"There is free interchange of products and a perfectly friendly feeling between the sister isles," said Mr. Oliphant. "The Irish have their parliament, at least their popular house in Dublin. The Senate which sits in London has the representatives of the four provinces into which Ireland is divided, who have an equal voice with the ten representatives for England, two for Wales, and four for Scotland."

"Are your Parliaments elected annually according to the Charter, so many points in which you have carried out, or triennially like the Australians, or septennially as in England of old? Then you have your President to elect also. I hope that is not as exciting a matter as it used to be in America!"

CHAPTER VI

"The President is elected once in six years, but that not by direct election. The Lower House is elected for three years, and is rarely dissolved till that term has expired, so that for a long time the Presidential election and the Commons election have been simultaneous. The President is elected by delegates from two hundred communes."

"Can a President be re-elected?"

"He may serve two terms. Our third President was chosen a second time."

"Were not people afraid to do this, lest it should become as permanent as royalty?" "He was extremely popular."

"If he dies in office?"

"There is no new election; he provides for a successor in that case, as also in case of serious illness or incapacitation for public business."

"Oh! I understand, as the Americans did. But you call this a Commonwealth out of compliment to the movement of the seventeenth century, I suppose."

"I think it was rather to distinguish between ourselves and the great transatlantic English speaking Republic."

"Why not call your President Protector, and keep up the distinction?"

"He does not protect us or the Commonwealth. We protect ourselves. We did not like that title."

I have already learned in the course of general conversation, that the President of the Commonwealth of Great Britain and Ireland, in the latter part of the year 1987, was a man who had worked his way up through commercial and provincial experience to the highest position in the country. He was a descendant, through his mother, of an eminent *savant* of my own day, but his father had belonged to the Artisan class. The probable successful candidate for the next term of office was a Guelph, a direct descendant of the Royal Family, who had made his mark in the new social order, and was now a leading member in the House of Commons. Royalty had ceased in England for nearly eighty years, but there were many descendants of the Empress Queen, as she was generally called, scattered over the world, and many of them in leading positions.

All the commercial and provincial assemblies were gratuitous, but both the Senate and the members of the House of Commons were paid for their services. But the modest salary of the President, and the allowance for the legislature, were no great strain on the industry of the people. As the legislature was paid, Mr. Oliphant told me that of course the sittings were held in the best part of the day--the morning. I told him that the Victorian paid legislature used to sit in the evening, which he said was exceptional.

I went into the House of Commons first. The building was the same but as the number was smaller, the great hall had been shorn of its vast proportions, and looked to me dwarfed, but it was easier to hear what was said. I listened to a debate and heard some good speaking, especially from Mr. Albert Guelph, but no impassioned eloquence. The minority of the day had their seats in the house; Mr. Guelph was at the head of the Opposition.

The question raised was as to immigration and emigration, and it was one which occasionally cropped up. In spite of the difficulty of obtaining employment in a society so thoroughly organised, where each man had his niche, and each niche its man, there was a tendency for people from the poorer continental countries, such as Germany, Russia, and Scandinavia, to turn to England. To allow free access to all-comers, who might take all risks and compete with the advanced society and bring down the standard of living, was dangerous. But yet I could not help sympathising with the feeling of the minority that something would be lost if a heavy poll-tax were imposed, or even the stronger measure suggested by Mr. Guelph. England had reached her old pre-eminence by being open to all-comers. A larger mixture of races than any continental nation possessed, had evolved a composite character with many of the best qualities of each, which liberty had strengthened by its being the refuge for the oppressed, where the most despotic Powers in Europe could not touch their political refugees. The dingy glories of Leicester Square were at an end, but Leicester Square had been a great factor in the triumph of free thought, free speech, and free action all over the civilised world.

The motion brought forward proceeded from what represented the Conservatives--England was to be kept for the English, and the English to be kept in England. So long as emigration and immigration were fairly balanced, things were to be as they were, but if immigration exceeded departures by 10,000 in one year, a heavy poll-tax was proposed. If, on the other hand, the emigration exceeded the arrivals by as many, an equivalent fine on departures was to be levied. This did not include travellers who only visited foreign countries, or visitors from the continent or from old colonies, who each had passports which did not allow them to settle or find employment. I was sorry to see the passport system in full swing in the twentieth century, but I was told that nothing else could have prevented England from being swamped by cheap labor at any time during the reconstruction and afterwards.

Emigration, in my time, had been looked on as the best and safest outlet for redundant population, and had indeed veiled for two or three generations the inexorable law of population from the average British intelligence. Now the idea seemed to be that of the Psalmist:

Dwell in the land, and there thou shalt be fed.

This bill was only in its second reading, and the debate was adjourned till the following week, when, of course, I could not know the issue.

There was much more State regulation and inspection than I had been used to, and the only parallel I could see approaching to it was the State legislation of the Western States of America; but this in England also was very much done by the provincial and communal bodies, so that the higher powers were relieved of much of the detail of administration. The nation, however, had Bureaus of Science, of Agriculture, of Meteorology, and seemed to make it its business to collect and formulate, and then to disseminate, all the information received, and all the discoveries made from year to year.

CHAPTER VI

The patent laws were changed so as to encourage invention, but as invention now-a-days was the fruit, not of a man's whole time, but of his abundant leisure, it was generally thrown into the common stock, though it was in every inventor's power to keep it for his own profit, or to sell it to someone who could make practical use of it.

In the Upper House there was a debate on a proposed extension of the Patent Law to ten years instead of five, but that was lost. The members of this Senate were older and few in number compared with the other. The President lived in Buckingham Palace during his term of office, and was fairly accessible. His wife was rather a homely woman, and, therefore, was not a leader of fashion.

The criminal statistics of the country were eminently satisfactory. Offences against the person were even rarer than those against the property, and these--owing to the industrial education of the people, and the openings for earning an honest livelihood, were wonderfully few. The elimination of the gambling spirit from business and from pleasure had removed many of the temptations to dishonesty.

Drunkenness, which though not punished by law either in the nineteenth or in the twentieth century, is at all times a fruitful parent of crime, was reduced so much by the temperate habits of a well-to-do and intelligent people, that this alone swept three-fourths of the cases out of the trial lists.

The Associated Homes with their gentle but continuous pressure have all but extinguished the drinking habits of old days, when hospitality and good-fellowship seemed to demand the liberal flow of intoxicating liquors to guests in the private house, or at the poor man's only drawing room, news room, and social club--the public-house.

The large amount of crime directly or indirectly traceable to illicit intercourse between the sexes was also minimised, if not stopped by the normal early marriages, which not only struck at vice, but the small families struck at poverty--another fruitful parent of crime. As illegitimate children had the same claims on the father as children born in wedlock, human-nature being what it is, marriage was preferred by the woman, and not objected to by the man. The mournful population checks of the past--cannibalism, infanticide, war, pestilence, and prostitution--were only spoken of as matters of history. The old Malthusianism of the past, which delayed the marriage of the prudent and thoughtful, while the reckless and improvident multiplied all the more, had resulted in the survival of the unfittest. This was especially noticeable when sanitary laws were better understood, and humanity and philanthrophy were eager to save the lives of the sickly and the defective, but took no steps to check their parenthood.

The neo-Malthusianism, of which I had barely heard, had, since my career had ended, taken hold of the world, beginning with the middle-classes, but rapidly embracing the more prudent and sensible of the artisan class, and gradually penetrating down to the lower class--the old so-called *proletariat*. It was by the severest restriction of charity, and by efforts--hitherto unparalleled--for the reclamation to industrial life of the more hopeful, and the younger of the class of tramps, vagrants and loafers, that these were at last forced to see that other people would no longer work to keep them in idleness. Whether these people possessed property, or not, now-a-days the old title of *proletariat* was no longer applicable, for they no longer produced large families.

Again out in the streets of London. It was unavoidable that much which Mr. Oliphant spoke of as real progress, should, to me, look like decay. There was not the tremendous rush and bustle I had been used to. The glory had gone off Regent-street and Old Bond-street, and many other fashionable streets in the West End. I missed the gaily set-out shop windows. I missed the jewellers' shops--the exquisite articles in silk, and lace, and furs, which only the wealthy could buy, but which all classes could admire.

Some trades stood their ground, and were carried on apart from co-operative stores, such as photography and dentistry, which both had expanded. There were comparatively few lawyers and doctors, and the clerical profession, as a means of livelihood, was conspicuous by its absence, but that large subject must stand over till Sunday.

"Two Chinese cities surpass it in population, and New York is considered more commercial, but it is rather difficult to calculate the

CHAPTER VI 122

wealth of a country where there are so few large accumulations, and where capital is not floating about in the hands of brokers and lent to nations, but employed actively in industrial undertakings. As a rule, a man's money goes with his work as a share of the concern. This makes a double bond to attach the workman to his industry, and gives to employment a permanence quite unknown in the preceding century."

Savings, I found, were made for old age and for the contingency of death while children were too young to provide for themselves. They were made in several ways, characteristic of the new society, in obtaining the freehold of the home, in not drawing out the dividends from the co-operative factories, but gaining a credit on their books, and in assurance societies proper, which dealt more in annuities after a certain age than in a lump sum at death.

Everyone having a margin over and above necessary expenditure, there was always some degree of inequality of wealth between those who spent and those who spared, but the gains of capital were small as compared to its proportion to labor in olden times, and capital was no longer what it had been, the arbiter of nations, the greatest power in the world socially as well as economically.

It is still powerful as increasing the powers of the human instrument incalculably, but it had settled down through its wide, almost universal distribution, to be a very cheap commodity.

The year's turn-over of money was really larger than it had been, for the population, but it no longer moved in such masses.

Mr. Oliphant thought New York was a richer city than London, and that one Australian city did not come far short of it.

The paper currency, which was national, like the railways, was based not entirely on gold, but on the State property in land and railways as well. The production of gold, which had been stimulated during the last years of the old *régime*, by its steady appreciation in value, had become smaller and smaller. A bi-metallic basis was introduced into most of the European nations as a stop-gap, but that was not

CHAPTER VI

satisfactory, and finally, other solid security was taken. So far as Mr. Oliphant and I could reckon it, the average income of the twenty-five millions of people inhabiting the Commonwealth of Great Britain and Ireland, a people, it must be remembered, of adults, employed productively in much larger proportion than in the nineteenth century, was nearly double what it was in the palmy days of free trade and unrestricted competition, when the enormous incomes of the millionaires were thrown into the balance. The purchasing power of money was in many directions less, and in some more. The length of the working life was the main factor in this extraordinary wealth.

I saw the inside of a jail, and of a lunatic asylum on this busy Friday. Harmless lunatics, after attempts for a cure had failed, often returned to their homes and were employed to the utmost of their capacities, chiefly out of doors. Criminal lunatics, such as those suffering from homicidal mania, were put to painless death. Those who had dangerous paroxysms, were kept safely and treated kindly, but employed during their lucid intervals.

Moral lunatics, or the residuum, which forms the permanent criminal class, were treated in much the same way, only that their work was of greater value, though it was conducted under costly inspection. One of the factors in national wealth was the comparatively small number of their failures.

The electric light, as I have already said, had superseded gas, both for domestic and street illumination. I saw London, both by daylight and by this effective substitute. The cleanliness of the city, its freedom from smoke, the open spaces, the liberal planting of trees, made it a very different city from the London of my recollections, but I began, as the day wore on, to feel at home in it. Yes, this was the place I really wanted to see most. I had made a right choice of the location for my short week. It was the central heart of the Commonwealth, it was, too, the ancient capital of all the daughter states which had been a-building so long. Here were preserved the archives, undestroyed, dating from before the Norman Conquest, which recorded the long growth of civilisation, liberty and orderly Government, which had been transplanted, with some modifications, to the ends of the earth. The mother-city of the van had not lost her historic glory through throwing

CHAPTER VI

off her surplus population.

Had England lost much in losing the great mixture of races, in educating power, or in her own national character? My friend thought the Englishman still equal, if not superior to the Anglo-Saxon of the Western or the Southern Hemispheres.

The English-speaking communities were still mindful of the fatherland. War having ceased all over the world, the alliance for peace or war which was held to be the main colonial bond in the nineteenth century was not needed; but the feeling between England and her daughter States, including the great Republic of America, was of the friendliest. Literature and laws, manners and customs, history and traditions were identically similar.

I felt more tired of this day's work than of any of the preceding, perhaps I now felt the accumulation of fatigue, carried over through taking in so many new ideas day after day.

There was a dance at the Owen Home every Friday evening, to which about twenty guests were invited--to add to the normal contingent of dancers. The children came in for one half-hour before going to bed; the grown people kept it up till nearly eleven. The dances were mostly new to me, and I thought graceful as well as decorous, and the music--like all I had heard in this newer England--admirable, and all furnished by the habitués of the music room.

I could not, however, sit out the whole series of dances, but retreated to my own room to write down what had struck me most of the day's sights and sounds. I note that even when I intend to keep to a certain department--such as politics and criminal law--the social question continually invades it. I never was very much of a politician--even my strong feeling in favor of what is called Hare's system of voting, which my nephews and nieces used to call Aunt Emily's fad, was less because it would give more equal representation to political parties than because it would strike at the root of the anti-social and immoral tendencies of the majority vote.

CHAPTER VI

I have always believed that people might be a great deal happier than they are, if they only managed their lives better, and if they did not make laws and follow customs which sacrificed the sick and the poor to the strong and the rich. Here, in the new society, the intelligent pursuit of happiness was the avowed object of all, and my curiosity as to the result of such an unusual pursuit was ever alert, and my kinsfolk--half amused, but wholly interested, were eager to satisfy me.

CHAPTER VII

SATURDAY

Literature and Art; Music; the Drama and Sport

How fast my week passed away. I rubbed my eyes at the sound of the awakening bell, and felt a new pang at the thought that this was my penultimate "Day in the Future." I had tried to follow some method in my researches. To-day I was not to travel much, but was to see the National Gallery, both of ancient and modern works of art, and the British Museum, and I was to try to form some estimate of the literature of the 20th century. The National Gallery, I found, had been enlarged enormously, and admirably classified and arranged, so that one could see as much or as little as one pleased. There were in it, stationed at various points, persons of both sexes who were thoroughly well informed as to the pictures and statues in their departments, who could give much fuller information than any catalogue. The light was well distributed. New modes of cleaning pictures had been adopted, and I could see that the old works of art were well preserved, and fairly appreciated. My attention, however, was mainly directed towards the later schools, and I was a little puzzled to know whether I preferred them to the more familiar styles of my own or of previous days. There were some striking pictures of the transition period between the age of competition and accumulation, and the communistic *régime* now established. There was not such savagery in the expression of the surging crowds who wrought this revolution as we were used to see in the pictures of the French Revolutionary period, but there was great intensity. A gallery of portraits of the leaders in the industrial reorganisation was interesting. I was delighted to know the names of many, some of my own day, and the sons and daughters of others whom I knew by reputation. There was a gallery of historical pictures connected with the cessation of war and of royalty all over Europe. These were fine; I thought, however, the later pictures were tame, except the landscape and sea-pieces, which were lovely in their fidelity to Nature, and yet you felt that Nature was seen through sympathetic human eyes. Photography--though it had made great progress--had not extinguished or even diminished artistic work, either in portraiture or in natural scenery. There was some good new sculpture, but Mr.

CHAPTER VII   127

Oliphant told me it was now impossible to get life models on hire. One might induce a friend to sit to him, but that was all. I was surprised at the progression of works of art of all kinds, especially as I heard that all considerable provincial towns had galleries of their own.

"How is it that so many devote themselves to art when your public are not rich enough to give their value for them?"

"Those who follow art for a livelihood are but few. Our artistic work is chiefly done in the leisure which everyone has, and these galleries are filled mainly with the gifts of the people to the people."

"That is, in one way, a pity, for art has always been understood to demand the strenuous study of a life-time. It is also the better for foreign travel, and for opportunities of seeing various styles."

"I do not know that we have the highest possible art; our connoisseurs point back to the old masters as unapproached by us, but we have an art that our people understand and appreciate. Our children, as you have seen, are early taught to observe form and color, light and shade, likeness and unlikeness, and to use the pencil and the brush; and if they have any talent, it shows itself. Our associated life allows the younger to obtain hints and corrections from the older. At our Owen Home there are many young people who work for hours every day in the art room. Of course, the best work is done in summer with the longer light. This gallery is open to students every day, and all day long."

"Dr. Johnson used to say of the Scotch that 'Every one had a mouthful of learning, but nobody had more'," said I.

"And you think it may be the same with our art? but the mouthful makes us happy, and I believe, makes us morally better than a perfect art, only understood by an upper ten thousand."

The British Museum had been also enlarged beyond all my expectations. There was nothing approaching to it in the Commonwealth or on the Continent of Europe for its comprehensiveness. The number of new books which had been

CHAPTER VII

published since I knew the world, was enormous. There were many readers in the museum--more than in my recollection of old times, though London was less populous. The Natural History and geological and other scientific collections were extensive and admirably arranged--with specialists able and willing to give information. The visitors were not the gaping crowds who knew nothing before and learned nothing then, but intelligent people who added to or fixed their previous acquisitions by what they saw and heard.

"I think I could read here," I said to Mr. Oliphant, as I sat down where I had sat more than a hundred and twenty years before, "nothing solid or demanding close attention, but let me see the sort of pabulum your young folks are nourished on--poetry and fiction."

"Here," said Mr. Oliphant, "are poems which I like, and which Florrie and her lover have read together in their brief courtship, and thought exquisite. It was Fred's gift-book to her; and here is a novel, or rather a novelette, of the day, very popular with the young. I shall go to my office and leave you here for two hours. I know you think our newspapers very inferior to the encyclopedian *Times* and the philosophical *Spectator* of your own day; and as you avoid the serious literature, you cannot see how the omissions of the daily and weekly press are supplied by books; but I may as well tell you that authorship, as a profession, is as rare as art. Our books are the product of our leisure, and rarely remunerate the writer. A very small royalty is all that the author claims, and no books are published at a high price. I do not dream of getting any profit by the book which I have had in hand for three years. Authorship is so delightful a thing that every one rushes into print who fancies he or she has anything to say. You note that we do not review books in the newspapers, and that they do not advertise with us; the task would be too great for us, the expense too great for the publishers."

When left alone I sat down and tried to do justice to the poems which were written by one who had been before the world for fifteen years. The verses were graceful and thoughtful, but I was in no way carried out of myself by them. It was easier for me to enter into the new life of the future, and to appreciate all the social arrangements by which life was made pleasanter, its sweetness and candor, its brightness and sympathy, than to be interested and amused by what delighted those around me. If the poems felt the touch of the level hand, how would the novel of contemporary life fare?

I think even worse. As early marriage was so easily entered into, the love embroglios (sic) were chiefly after marriage, and had much to do with divorce. The custody of children was a point settled by arbitration of friends, but the party who appeared most to blame in the separation had the worse position, and often this led to reconciliation. I really could not keep my attention closely fixed on the loves of Nigel and Elaine, interrupted by a twentieth century villain, but all brought to a happy conclusion, but I could see that the little boy had a great deal to do with it.

I was told by my friends that there was another school of fiction resembling the historical romance which was very popular, and another purely ideal, in which spirits and fairies and supernatural beings, the belief in whom had quite died out, were called out to paint a moral and adorn a tale. The metrical tale was very popular, as also the ballad to be read or to be sung. There were some magazines, both of light and serious literature, but not so many as I left in the world. The cessation of advertisements had probably killed many of them. The newspapers confined themselves to their own department, and did not publish serial stories to induce a large circulation. If people wanted stories and poetry they had to buy them in books, but the writers had increased in a larger proportion than the buyers, because the Homes and the syndicates of Homes made one copy of a book do more duty than the old circulating libraries.

I saw some athletic sports and games of various kinds that Saturday afternoon to show me how the young people took their out-door amusements. Admission to cricket and such matches was free.

"You have as yet seen none of our public entertainments," said Mrs. Oliphant to me. "What would you prefer, the theatre, the concert room, or the opera?"

"Have you actually an opera? I should have thought that was a luxury only possible where there was a wealthy community. If there is really

CHAPTER VII

opera, I should prefer that, and if possible, in old Covent Garden."

"That is our Opera House, and there is a new and, I hear, a fine piece in representation there at present. As for opera being unsuited to our condition of social equality, almost everyone is musical enough to appreciate it, and as the stars do not now swallow up half the profits, we have very even talent all round, and the entertainment is not costly."

We did not get the best seats, because these were obtained by prior engagement, and our minds were made up too late for that, but we did not get the worst because we were at the doors early. Italian opera at one shilling and one and sixpence could not be called dear, and before I had heard a quarter of the overture I felt satisfied it would be in no way inferior. The libretto, which I glanced over in advance, seemed better than I recollected reading in old days. The scene of the opera was laid in the time of revolution and reconstruction, and Mrs. Oliphant told me it was as true to history as so artificial a thing as opera could be made. The title was "The last of the Czars," and it showed how the absolute autocrat was driven to abdication by the pressure of his rebellious subjects. There were mobs and barricades, armies and battles; the disused arms I had seen and others invented after my day were brought forward to show what life had been. The sycophants, the parasites, and the spies who flattered the monarch up to the turn of fortune, and then deserted and betrayed him, were shown up, and what was, perhaps, more difficult, the more honest but equally mischievous blood and thunder veterans who accounted that the end--the preservation of the empire--justified all means of repression and cruelty to individuals and classes. On the other hand were the prophets and apostles, the workers and the fighters in the cause of freedom and progress, animating peasants to action, and undermining the plots of the powerful. The returned exiles from Siberia who took such a prominent part in the revolution, were wild and haggard and neglected in their attire, but full of passionate eloquence. The Russian national airs, with their pathetic music, were introduced with excellent effect. I was as thoroughly carried away with the drama of the future as I had been when I heard Ristori and her company act Marie Antoinette. I was living in the story and I lost myself in the music.

CHAPTER VII

During the intervals I looked at the audience. The electric light showed tier on tier of interested and intelligent spectators. There was no dress circle--in fact, there was no such thing as full dress in twentieth century society. People went in their ordinary clothes--their better clothes, no doubt--with a little show of ribbons on the part of the women and natural flowers worn by both sexes. There was no crowd of carriages at the door of the Opera House. Only a few of such vehicles as belonged to the Owen Home for the older and more infirm who wanted to be present. Although the audience was most appreciative, there were no *encores*. The opera, indeed, was a long one, but I understood from Mrs. Oliphant that *encores* were out of fashion. There was no calling before the curtain till the close of the performance, when the performers received a shower of flowers. The dresses of the company were tasteful, but not costly, that of the peasants and the exiles and refugees most satisfactory in their appropriateness. Close behind us, there sat a Russian gentleman, known to Mr. Oliphant, who came from a backward province in Siberia, and who had come to spend a year in England to study agriculture. He was deeply interested in this national drama that he had just missed hearing in St. Petersburg.

"I fear you must always go backward to find material for anything like a plot," said I. "Your present times are too level and too prosperous for picturesque artistic treatment."

"True, for the sensational and exciting we must go back, but we have a domestic drama that interests us. So long as people differ in character and temper, so long will their story present something for genius to take hold of. But no doubt genius is very glad of the varied resources of the past."

"Is your opera a co-operative affair, like so many other concerns now-a-days? Or is it as it used to be with us--the speculation of an *impresario* who engaged his troupe and made the profit, or submitted to the loss of the season?"

"It is so far co-operative that everyone, down to the most insignificant chorus-singer and scene-shifter, has a share in the receipts, but there is a head who conducts all the business, and a joint stock company who furnish the capital. London has this company for four months in

CHAPTER VII   132

the year. They travel through the provinces for the rest of the year, often dividing into two bands, where the houses are too small for the whole strength of the company. There is an oratorio company who devote themselves in the same way to sacred compositions."

"Your London population is so small now, it is little larger than the London of Johnson and Garrick, when Drury Lane and Covent Garden supplied all the legitimate drama."

"The population, though comparatively small, is much more stationary than the well-to-do used to be, and all our people are more pleasure-loving than the average Englishman of old times."

"It used to be the visitors--the country cousins--who kept up the theatres in London, and in Paris, too. You have not got so many visitors now."

"We have more than you fancy, but not at harvest time--the busiest time of the year in the country. The balance now is against London, for many are on their country holiday. But our people are all fond of music and the drama. Everyone has some spare money and a good deal of spare time. Even the constant amateur performances which we have in our Homes increase our taste for them, and make us desire to see the same thing done better so that we may obtain valuable hints. The next act, Miss Bethel, opens with a dance. I am glad that it will give you an idea of our ballet-dancing."

It was lovely--the very poetry of motion with nothing of the objectionable features of nineteenth century stage-dancing. I have before said that the dress in the future was not rigorously of one mode. The young and active wore shorter skirts than the older, and many preferred a modification of the Bloomer costume--the belted tunic and full drawers. This last was the favorite dress of the ballet-dancers, and their sleeves were worn half-long. If paint and pearl powder was still used on the stage, it was used judiciously, but, probably, the full glare of the electric light required some make-up in this way. The audience, I felt sure, had only their natural complexions.

CHAPTER VII

It is rather hard work to take stock of everything seen and heard during each day of my week every night, and I think I feel more puzzled to appraise the literature than anything else. I fancy one must have lived up to the times to enjoy their literary flavor. It is far easier to go back, for we have, through our ancestors, through our traditions, through our historical studies, learned in a measure to throw off the present, and thus we can enter, in imagination, into a world where the railway, the telegraph, the penny post, and the household franchise, were unknown and undreamed of. One can sit down with Samuel Johnson, or with Addison, or with Milton, and feel in what a world they lived and worked.

We can go back further still, to the troubled life of Dante or the cloister of St. Bernard, or even to the classic times of Greece or Rome. But in the hundred years that had elapsed since I had known the world, first had come a cataclysm sweeping away the old foundations and much that had been reared on them, and from these had gradually emerged a new society which I had been only a week engaged in studying. No longer were the prizes of life held by the few through inheritance, or snatched by energy, by business talent, by unscrupulous rapacity, or by subtle craft. No more startling rises and falls in social position, no more apparently respectable people drifting into crime, on the pressure of fierce temptation arising from opportunities which no longer were given, and the precariousness of a position which seemed to depend entirely on money. Mr. Oliphant reminded me that a crusader of the twelfth century, a feudal lord of the thirteenth, a border raider of the fifteenth, and a buccaneer of the sixteenth, would have thought our nineteenth century tame and uneventful, for in it law was mightier than the sword, and violence was put down by the stronger hand of the policeman. To ourselves our own times will always be interesting, and to photograph ourselves in our habit as we live must always be a pleasing spectacle to the living generation. So far, however, as I am able to judge, and I do not pretend to be anything but an amateur, or a *dillitante* (sic), or any other word that connotes my insufficient knowledge of art, I thought the nineteenth century newspapers, poetry and novels, were better and, to me, more interesting than those of the future. Mr. Oliphant regretted I had not time to study history and science, which he said I should find had made great advances. He also felt now that if I lived longer with the *post-nati*, I should like the other outcomes of their spirit, better too. I completely gave in as to

CHAPTER VII

music. I was not so sure as to painting. Humor I thought was much less developed than in my own time. There were far fewer absurd people in the world, and there was not the same ridiculous difference between our aims and our accomplishments, between a man's estimate of himself, and that which other people form of him that amuses lookers-on now-a-days. There was, of course, the thoughtless laughter of children in abundance, and the high spirits of youth, but that subtle quality of humor, that consoling spirit that has softened the disparities of life, has soothed the sorrows and the disillusions of the nineteenth century was very slightly apparent in such intercourse as I had with my successors. Some of the best people of the world in all ages have had little or no sense of humor. I think I was especially drawn to Mr. Oliphant because with him it was stronger than with others whom I met.

And how did my new friends look on me? Kindly enough, but with some pity that I had been placed in such a barbarous age. Yet this barbarous age contained in it the germs of all that had been accomplished afterwards. It was the beginning of the age of conscious evolution. Before my day the race had stumbled forward, fighting blindly, struggling manfully for life. In common with thousands, nay with tens-of-thousands, I had entered the epoch of consciousness, the open-eyed, dignified manhood of humanity. We had power and passion, we only paused for knowledge, so as to apply these to the good and happiness of all. I looked back, and I saw the beginning of much that had been evolved in my own mind, and in the minds of others. I, myself, had done something, not much, but still somewhat towards those changes that others had worked more efficiently under more favorable circumstances to bring about.

CHAPTER VIII

SUNDAY

Religion & Morality

"For to-day," said my friend, Mr. Oliphant, "I think it would be well to put you under the care of St. Bridget, who knows more of the religious life of our modern society than I can pretend to do. But this I must premise that in the most extraordinary way religion has showed its vitality. The old historical Christianity was assailed from all quarters. You must recollect that in your own day scientific discoveries and critical studies of the Bible shook the faith of many. But that was nothing to the great mass of infidelity which preceded and accompanied the social revolution which you were expecting--that catastrophe which closed your century and introduced ours. The Meliorists were not all unbelievers, for in every Church in the world there were many who devoutly hoped and trusted that God himself would redress wrongs, and bring in a sort of miraculous millenium; but the active spirits--the Socialists, the Communists, and the Nihilists--were impassioned and aggressive Secularists and looked on the churches as the greatest hindrances in the way of human progress. As the world settled down after the revolution, these Secularist leaders were surprised to find that the churches were not deserted--as they had confidently expected, but that large numbers of the new generation, rising up, clung to the faith in the unseen and the unknown. Worship appears to be a necessity for the average human nature, but, with every advance in knowledge and in morality, comes a change in the ideas we have of the Being whom we worship, and of the services which is acceptable to Him. The constancy of the natural laws, or rather of the natural order, is now too firmly established to allow of prayer for definite blessings being offered. Prayer with us is adoration of a Power felt to be ten-thousand times greater than was dreamed of by Psalmist or Apostle, and aspiration after such perfection as is open to a humanity no longer under a curse, no longer finding its only salvation in fetters or leading-strings, but free to seek after the best and the highest."

"Then are the Churches stronger than they used to be?"

CHAPTER VIII

"They are stronger, in that they have let go their weaker defences, but they are not nearly so strong in numbers as you recollect them. There are still very many sceptics in the world, but the age of scoffers is over. Honest sceptics are acknowledged to have done good service in the past, and to do good service in the present, even by the most devout among us. Religion being now absolutely free, neither endowed nor supported by the State, is a matter between a man's conscience and his God, there is no longer a premium on hypocrisy, and there is no vantage ground occupied by it, either pecuniarily or socially."

"Is there then no priestly caste or class now-a-days?"

"No; none at all."

"Are there no men and women--I see from Miss Somerville that women are included--brought up for the ministry? They used to have this special training, even for dissenting congregations in my day. It was considered that such an education and the devotion of the whole life were needed to make any ministry effective."

"We consider the ordinary education of the citizen is the best foundation, and the ordinary life the best preparation."

"Then is the public worship of the faithful a mere matter of chance, those speaking whom the Spirit moves, as among the venerable Society of Friends."

"Not altogether. Our religious teachers have something superadded in the way of study, though there is great latitude given to outsiders in most denominations."

"Ah! now I understand. This spiritual ministration--like almost all your literature and art--is the work of that leisure which is so equally possessed by all classes of society, all grades of intelligence and all varieties of temperament."

"Just so. If Paul, who had the conversion of a whole heathen world on his hands, could earn his daily bread by his avocation of a tent-maker, surely the building up of the faithful in the modern spiritual temple might be accomplished by the many devout souls who have provided things honest in the sight of all men by their work during the week. Naturally permanent charges corresponding to the old parishes and congregations fall to those who are most fitted for it, but help and variety are obtained from others."

"Lay brothers and sisters, I suppose?"

"There is no lay, when there are no clerics," said Mr. Oliphant; "but there is a large body of the unattached, who assist the regular ministrants."

"And St. Bridget belongs to the regulars?"

"Yes, or she could not have joined Fred and Florrie in marriage together. She preaches very well, but her special gift is prayer. We could not afford to shut out quite half of the piety of the world from the ministry by making our women keep silence in the churches."

"In spite of Paul?"

"We owe no slavish obedience to a temporary instruction of Paul, even if that was what he meant, and not to stop idle questions and interruptions of Divine service."

"Are you a church-goer yourself, Mr. Oliphant?"

"Occasionally. Not regularly."

"It is still respectable to go to church? I suppose."

"Yes; but quite as respectable to stay at home, if you do not feel that it does you good."

"Then, if the intolerance of the churches, with regard to sceptics, has been softened, what of the intolerance and aggressiveness of the sceptics towards the churches?"

CHAPTER VIII

"That is also changed. The churches are not now maintained at great cost to the public. They neither persecute nor taboo non-believers, and, therefore, their attitude disarms aggression. But I must now hand you over to St. Bridget. I am going to have a good day over my book, all the better, I believe, for the week's talk with you."

Miss Somerville had an engagement to conduct public worship in the evening, but for the morning she was free. I took her completely into my confidence, and I found her more ready to believe my strange story than even my own kinsfolk.

"Where do you wish to go to?" she asked.

"Either to St. Paul's or Westminster Abbey, preferring the latter. We are too late for early service, so the forenoon must be our time."

"Westminster Abbey, like a great many churches of all denominations, stands open all Sunday, and is open for morning and evening service every day."

"That is a good borrowing from the Roman Catholic Church, which the Anglican resembles in many respects."

"Other churches do the same. The church is now understood to be more a house of prayer than a preaching place."

"Are the denominations as numerous as they used to be?"

"Not nearly so numerous. Many have merged minor differences and taken a broad platform for united action."

"Such as the various forms of Methodism, for example?"

"Yes, these have merged in one body. Others, such as the Congregationalists and Baptists have united, both believing in adult baptism only. Infant baptism distinguishes these from the united body of Presbyterians, to whom I am bound by ancestry, but baptism of this kind is now a simple dedication service."

CHAPTER VIII

"Have the High Church Anglicans and the Roman Catholics abandoned the miraculous element in the baptismal service and the sacraments generally?" said I, in the greatest surprise.

"We hear less and less about it as the years roll on. Common sense has attacked it from one side, and from the other we learn that spiritual influences are immanent from the Deity, and not obtained by any jugglery with material things, even by what were called sacramental elements."

"Then there is no social advantage or prestige in belonging to the English Church now-a-days, nor any heart-burnings among those who remain outside of it."

"When the establishment and the temporalities fell, the edge and the bitterness of dissent were taken off."

"What training do your ministers receive to fit them for the position they have to fill?" "Each denomination has its own standard. The scholarship may vary, but piety is thought indispensable."

"And as the employment is entered into without hope of reward, there is no temptation for such as have no vocation to enter into it."

"I gave three years of my leisure to theological study, and then had three years probationary work before I took such orders as are needed for the care of a congregation." "And this, too, is the work of your leisure. In my time the whole life was given to it." "Given to what?" asked St. Bridget, simply.

"To parochial and ministerial duties."

"What did these include?"

"Conducting public worship and preaching twice on Sunday and often on weekdays besides. In the Catholic and the High Anglican Churches there was morning and evening prayer besides. There was superintending the Sunday Schools, catechising the young, visiting the sick and the dying, platform work, and generally keeping up social intercourse with the flock."

"Well, you will see and hear our services to-day. We have no week-day services except morning and evening prayer, conducted by probationers and other volunteers in training for the ministry, which, itself, is only a larger offering of voluntary service."

"Mr. Oliphant tells me that you pay none of your religious teachers."

"Not one. Except for the repair of churches which were our inheritance from the past, there is no expense connected with our religious services."

"Your organists and choir?"

"Give their services as their offering."

"Your church cleaners and pew openers, if such still exist?"

"These also offer their work without payment."

"God forbid that I should make an offering to my God of that which costs me nothing," said I, quoting David.

"Exactly so!" said St. Bridget, "that is what the devout feel. They delight to give of their time, and their care, and their thought, and their prayers, and would feel hurt if they were paid in money or a money's worth for them."

"But what of the community which accepts this?"

"We learn to accept much from our brethren now-a-days. If each gives his best for the general good, as you have seen, I am sure in other departments, surely the devout need not hang back. Most of us are poorer than the average citizen, because we are tempted to borrow from the hours which are given to self-supporting work for this labor we delight in. This is the only asceticism possible to us in these times."

CHAPTER VIII

"The clergy of all denominations had great care of the poor a century ago. In North and East London, and in the great manufacturing towns the demands on the time and the purse of ministers of religion were enormous. Countless schemes for the relief and the improvement of the masses were originated or furthered by them, and many were the disappointments they met with in this difficult work of charity."

"That branch of duty is saved them now-a-days."

"How do you read Christ's saying--'The poor ye have always with you." Do you consider it to be only a local and temporary justification of the splendid lavishness of the devout woman?"

"In the old material sense it is not true now, but it was with Christ's weapons and in Christ's spirit (though often unconsciously) that we virtually annihilated poverty. Who that saw the grand self-sacrifice, the absolute dedication of the noblest souls to the reconstruction of society, could doubt the source of the movement? But there are always poorer and richer intellectually, and especially spiritually, and it is for those who are more highly endowed to aid and encourage the lower and weaker souls. Our whole framework of society rests on that bearing of each other's burdens which is helpful to all. Every man, no doubt, bears his own burden in another sense. Our individual souls have to account to our Creator for the course they have run, the light they have shed, or the light they have closed themselves to, or intercepted from others."

"I have been feeling that there seems little or nothing for good, and pious, and energetic, people to do. In my time the amount to be done was enormous, though, I confess, that much of our efforts seemed wasted through our own ignorance and through the weakening of the self-reliant spirit in those we wished to serve. Still, it was for the time gratified activity, which was to our happiness. But now--"

"I can see you are somewhat depressed by what seems to you a dead level of uniformity. To me there appears infinite variety. I feel not only with strangers, but with the hundred or more who inhabit the Owen Home, such contrasts, such gradations of character, and every now and then (well as I know them) I have surprises--things that were quite

CHAPTER VIII 142

unlooked-for--either good or bad."

"Everything is comparative," said I. "As Mr. Oliphant says, the nineteenth century would have appeared colorless and flat to the feudal chiefs of the twelfth century, or to the buccaneers of the sixteenth. To me it was in many ways painful, but it was intensely interesting. I fear you have forgotten it and its struggles."

"No one who thinks at all can fail to be grateful to the men and women of that century who saw sympathetically what was the value of humanity. It was a prophecy not far from its fulfilment."

"And what of its scientific spirit and the long-continued battle it maintained with the creeds of the churches?"

"A battle, from which both came out victorious. The churches were shaken to their old foundations, and came out purified and spiritualised. A century which severed the connection between Church and State, which saw the destruction of the Pope's temporal power, the source of one-half of the evils under which the Catholic world groaned, and which reorganised that ancient church on surer foundations, which inaugurated general national education, and which, after great bandying of the words, Religious and Secular, as war cries, at last settled their just boundaries. Ah! we, of the religion, owe much to that shaking!"

"All the devout, in my day, were alarmed at the secular tendencies of the age, especially in the matter of education."

"With me, and those who feel with me, there is nothing secular. Every thing is profoundly religious. I do not believe there is not an Associated Home in the Commonwealth where there is not one--or more than one--who gives religious teaching to the little ones, not on Sundays only, but every day. We follow them to the National Schools, we do not leave them at the continuation schools. It is no part of the State-paid teachers' work, but it is the privilege of our volunteers."

"But do not many sceptical parents object to your giving instruction of which they disapprove?"

CHAPTER VIII

"Very few of them go so far as that, though if they do, we respect their wishes." "And does this make all your people grow up pious?"

"No; certainly not. The proportion of professing Christians is much smaller than in your day; but no one professes one thing and believes another. After all, sincerity is the first of virtues."

"But Rome and its mighty hierarchy? Do you mean to tell me that money does not enter into the relations between priest and people? Why, it was not the maintenance of the clergy that the devout Catholic paid for, it was the saving of his own soul and the souls of those dear to him from purgatorial fires!"

"The first step in the purification of the older Christian Church was the destruction of the temporal power, and making the Pope merely the spiritual head of the church, freeing him from the entanglements and the limitations of an ordinary reigning sovereign. His spiritual power became greater than it had been for centuries. When all other churches relinquished their temporalities, Rome had to follow suit. No church ever contained more devout and devoted souls, and, as a rule, the best religious work had always been done for nothing. It was the salt of the volunteer work that saved the mass from utter putrefaction. It still proclaims itself infallible, indivisible, and unchangeable, but it has, in fact, maintained its authority and its prestige by adapting itself to the new conditions of society."

"And what of the celibacy of the clergy?"

"That is maintained, as well as that of many working brothers and sisters, but all these earn their livelihood like other people, a little more meagre, generally, because, as I have said, the spiritually-minded want more for their special work than the ordinary leisure of the citizen."

"I see another cause of the great average wealth of the community, which has so much astonished me. Your religious teachers are natural producers, and not maintained at the cost of the industry of others."

CHAPTER VIII

"We find that much of what used to be stigmatised as ecclesiastical narrowness has disappeared, since our religious teachers ceased to be a clerical caste. Mr. Oliphant often tells me that my caps and bonnets possess the balance of my intellect--in fact, keep me sane."

"I hope that the Greek Church has been influenced in the same way as the Roman, and that the domination of an ignorant and arrogant priesthood has been exchanged for the helpfulness of an enlightened and sympathetic ministry."

"It was only suffered to exist on such conditions. The Russian Revolutionists thought they could destroy the Church as they had destroyed the throne, but they found themselves mistaken. The mass of the people felt religion to be a necessity of their nature."

When we reached Westminster Abbey I was glad to find we were early, and I watched the congregation as it arrived--a plainly-dressed, reverent, and apparently devout body of men, and women, and children. The prayer book had undergone a considerable amount of excision and addition. These happy, contented worshippers no longer called themselves miserable sinners, or entreated the Good Lord to spare them, as if but for their anguished petitions hell and destruction were ready to swallow them up. As children, to a father, they came with their thanks and their desires, knowing that He loved them, and that if their souls were laid open to Him, His spirit of goodness and of peace would flow in upon them. There were pious words of mediaeval saints and of later worthies introduced into the prayers; some, quite new to me, about which St. Bridget informed me afterwards. The hymns were mostly new. I regretted this, because I wished, so much, to recall my own early religious feelings and traditions in that part of the service in which I could actively join. But I could not help seeing, with pleasure, that the musical part of the service all through was congregational.

From every corner swelled the notes of praise. No professional choir did that service for the worshippers, but hymn and anthem belonged to all. The responses were mostly musical, but when not so, were simultaneous, and not following a leader. Beautiful music had surrounded every child from the day of his birth: it was like the air he

CHAPTER VIII

breathed, so everyone seemed to sing, and to sing true in the twentieth century. The reading was also excellent, and not intoned, but natural.

The subject of the sermon I heard in Westminster Abbey was the "rich young ruler," in Matthew xix, who sought to know what good thing he should do that he might have eternal life. The answer of Christ was "If thou wilt enter into life, keep the commandments." He said, "Which?" and Jesus said "Thou shalt do no murder; Thou shalt not commit adultery; Thou shalt not steal; Thou shalt not bear false witness; Honor thy father and thy mother; and, Thou shalt love thy neighbor as thyself." All, it may be observed, duties to our neighbors. The entrance into life depended on the discharge of them. But, if thou wilt be perfect, "Go, sell all that thou hast, and give to the poor, and come follow me" The counsel of perfection, as the Catholic Church often calls it, meant the sharing of inherited or acquired wealth with those who had nothing, and the devotion of this life to the spread of the Gospel. The young ruler was able to do the first, but not to rise to the higher level. A vivid picture of the old disparities of life was drawn, and Christ represented less as the mediator between God and man than as the mediator between the rich and strong in this world, and their poorer and weaker brethren.

Terror, with regard to the unseen and the unknown, seemed to have completely passed away. In the case of Miss Somerville, belief in the personal God, in the gracious Redeemer, in the ever immanent Spirit, and the conscious immortality of the Soul was as strong as it could have been in the so called ages of faith, but it was combined with the most perfect confidence that those who did not share her faith might share its blessings. The theological beliefs of the past had aided in evolving conscience; the religious organisations still had it as their task to direct and to strengthen conscience and to gather up all the tender and reverent feelings of the religious nature of man, and, while doing so, allied all their religious feelings to the cause of truth and progress.

If in former times St. John's had been the favorite Gospel of the devout, it was now Luke who was the greatest authority. In his Gospel, and in the Acts of the Apostles, were found much fore-shadowing of the recent changes in society. Christ was regarded as the prophet and

CHAPTER VIII

pioneer of the social order so long delayed, when each member of the human family should feel for every other member. Mistake and misapprehension, violence, ambition and greed, had kept back the unfolding of the Gospel germ for nearly two thousand years, but to Christ all Christian socialists, and even many sceptical socialists looked back with gratitude and reverence. Morality and religion were inextricably woven together. The Fatherhood of God was apprehended and understood through the brotherhood of man.

Although so many churches were open all day, the Sunday was not kept rigidly sacred. On Sunday afternoons most of the young people were out of doors, and many of them engaged in such relaxations as I had seen on the Saturday afternoon. Miss Somerville spent it in reading of a devotional character preparatory to an evening service which she conducted, to which I went with her in a small church not far from the Owen Home. She took as her subject Communion with God, and I could see that she would indeed have been a mystic, if she had lived in a darker age. She was penetrated with the Divine, but yet her daily life kept her in touch with the Human.

I asked her if she did not, in some ways, regret the past of which she had made a study, and the heroes and heroines, the saints and ascetics, of the churches whom she loved and admired so much.

"No," said she, "by no means. Surely the God whom we all worship, more or less ignorantly, must be better pleased with a world in which there is less prayer but more happiness, and less cruelty, oppression and greed. Can there be any praise sweeter to our Heavenly Father than the happy unchecked laughter of children, the hopeful ardor of youth, the earnest endeavors of mature years, the placid contentment of old age? We no longer look on Him as the Lord of Hosts, the arbiter of battles, as our ancestors did, but we see that the millenial peace dreamed of by pious souls in all ages has fallen upon the earth. Woman is no longer degraded as the slave or the toy of man, but takes her equal place in all relations of life. No child is crushed beneath the wheels of the Juggernaut car of commercial prosperity or ascendancy. The distinctions of caste are obliterated. The slave is free, the serf is his own master, the laborer eats in peace and security the fruits of his toil. Surely now, if ever in the history of our earth, the Lord may look on

CHAPTER VIII

the things that he has made and pronounce them 'very good.'"

My week has come to an end. Short though it has been, it has been full of interest, full of all that I have accounted life. A good exchange for a year or two of mere existence.

"Now, Lord, let Thy servant depart in peace, now that I have seen the salvation wrought by brotherhood for the families of the earth."

THE END

A free ebook from http://manybooks.net/

Printed in Great Britain
by Amazon